Gennita Low

SEX LIES & SPIES serials

SHORT VIGNETTES IN THE LIVES OF SPIES.

EACH NOVELLA OF THIS SERIES IS AN EPISODE SHOWING
SECRET MOMENTS BRINGING TWO SPIES TOGETHER

THE GAME

Advantage. *The first move, by White, begins with a slight advantage in time.*

Small advantage. *An advantage so insignificant that the opponent sometimes doesn't even realize it is an advantage. Accumulation of small advantages leads to a winning attack.*

CHAPTER ONE

John Dallas adjusted his binoculars. Scowled. Adjusted them again.

"Well, I'll be damned," he muttered softly, so no one could actually hear his words. His horse moved restlessly at the sound of his voice. His displeasure must have somehow conveyed itself to the man on horseback beside him.

"Do you not like what you see, Johan?" the man spoke in accented English, using the Muslim variation of John's name. "I assure you she comes from good stock. Maybe your European schooling has made you unused to her clothing, but I have been told she is pleasing to look at."

The last sentence was spoken loudly, so the others behind them could listen in, if they chose. John snorted, his eyes glued to the binoculars. He knew what the man was trying to do—make sure he didn't forget he had a role to play. As if he could. His grip tightened as he surveyed the approaching group of people.

His companion obviously didn't like that reaction, because he started speaking in his native Pakistani dialect hurriedly. "She is a little old, but that's because she, unlike most village women, has been to school. But that's what you demanded, that she be educated. And you agreed that her dowry is what you wanted."

Yeah, amazing how they came up with the perfect candidate. He'd thought his request almost impossible, but as always, the powers-that-be had a way to make things happen. He reined in his temper and put away the binoculars. He pulled at the collar of his garment. It was stifling hot and he wanted out of these Pakistani sacks. He wanted to be back in the States. So the faster he went through with this, the quicker he would be able to demand an explanation.

He didn't quite know how the hell he'd gotten into this mess. One minute he was just negotiating for a unique exchange. The next, he found out he was part of it.

He gritted his teeth, then tried to pass it off as a smile to reassure his increasingly alarmed companion. "Everything is well, Hashem," he told the man. He couldn't afford to make anyone nervous right now. They were being watched, he was pretty sure of it. "She looks exactly as I'd imagined."

Indeed she did. There was no mistaking the face, even though the rest of her was swathed in those black umbrella-shaped garments in which the people here imprisoned their women. Heart-shaped. Small nose. A mouth made for a man's fantasy.

John couldn't believe that this was happening to him. She was his dream woman. A killer dream that visited him whenever he let down his guard. A witch who wouldn't let go of his balls. A master manipulator.

And he was marrying her today.

***

All around them were mountains. They had traveled four days to reach this particular spot and everyone was

5

dusty and tired. It certainly was not the usual way to meet a wedding contingent. The groom-to-be sat on his black horse, looking expectantly in the direction of the approaching group of people.

The men behind him, at some given signal, started clapping their hands in unison, a sign of welcome in these parts. One had to make noise to show approval; silence meant confrontation. They also knew there were eyes in these mountain parts, eyes that reported anything out of the ordinary.

The arriving contingent rode over the slope, trotting at a moderate pace, and finally came to a slow halt not far from the waiting camp. John and his friend, the only ones on horseback, rode to meet them. They ignored the heat as they studied the other group.

The waiting men in the other group eyed the tall one on the black mare, perfectly aware which of them was the leader. Dressed like that, in traditional garb, he looked like one of them, black hair and fierce dark eyes that assessed everyone.

"*Salaamua'laikum*. Welcome," John said, "brothers."

"Not yet," the one in front replied, a bite to his voice.

John lifted an enquiring brow. "Of course. Whenever you are ready."

"Do you have what we asked for?" This was spoken in a low voice.

John leaned forward on his horse. From afar, it looked like a warm gesture, brother to brother. "As long as you have what I want," he answered cryptically, giving a passing glance to the cart that had stopped behind them. It was pulled by two donkeys, and flanked by men on each side. "Which one of the women is mine?"

The tribesman's smile was very white against his dark tan. Tall, broad-shouldered, with intelligent dark eyes, his English was perfect New York. He struck an imposing figure, machine gun hanging loosely on one side, a broad sword on the other. Gold flashed in his ear. With the mountain backdrop, he looked as if he stepped out of another time, a warrior ready for battle.

"The one staring back at you," he told John. "She can speak English, cook, sew, and dance. Just a little too old, and thus a little disobedient. Not what our village men usually go for. What do you think?"

John looked over the man's shoulder. His intended was certainly being disobedient, daring to stare at her future husband straight in the eye. At least she wasn't smiling. He nudged his horse to turn around, gesturing for the others to follow. "She will do."

***

An old maid's wedding wasn't anything more than a quick handshake in these parts of the world. The woman would be grateful, glad to find someone to take care of her. Her relatives would be relieved. Unmarried women in villages were frowned upon, unless they were maids or nannies.

So the man and the woman joined hands under the stern eye of an *imam* and a cloudless sky, and that was it. There was the marriage tent, staked for the night while the witnesses gathered outside to make a record of the event. The men drank sweet coffee and sang. The women held their own party inside a separate tent. A gentle mountain breeze streamed through the camp, and the atmosphere became slightly more relaxed.

The newly married wife carried a jug of water from a nearby stream, and waited by the front flap of the tent for her new husband. He was in the men's tent, signing documents, taking note of what she came with.

She couldn't quite believe that he'd actually gone through with the marriage, but of course, he had no choice. He needed her dowry.

A reasonable time must pass before her husband could come to her. She was no young maiden and he was no eager youth clamoring after his first wife. The Muslims, she noted, were allowed four. At her age, she supposed, she was remarkably fortunate to be the first. The last thought was made with her usual sarcastic sense of humor, something no one here knew existed.

Well, no one, except her husband. He knew.

And he would be exacting revenge as soon as they entered their tent that night. Sizzling anticipation thrummed through her, even as she stood waiting just outside their tent, serene as the first light of dawn.

Male voices mingled with the approaching darkness. Torches were lit. She smelled the food. She heard the soft whinnying of the resting horses. The cooling mountain air was welcoming. Somehow she hadn't quite envisioned her wedding day to be quite like this. Shrouded. Alone. Waiting like a supplicant.

Her husband suddenly appeared before her, a menacing figure in his robes, six feet two inches of masculine power. She waited till he paused in front of her, close enough that she caught the scent of man and horse. She'd been waiting for this moment all day. Longer than that, actually. Bending down, she picked up the large jar of water. On cue, her husband sat down on the stool she had readied. Not a word passed between them.

She knelt down, placed the jug close by, and slowly unshod him, first one foot, then the other, before starting the traditional footbath a married man in these parts received before entering his abode. It was an honor a newly wedded woman bestowed on her man.

His tension was evident in the way his calf muscles were clenched. It was dark enough to allow her to explore him more curiously than was proper, and she moved her fingers boldly and slowly over the top of one foot. She palmed the arch of the other as she poured water over it, taking her time as she ran her thumb around the sensitive pads under the toes. Leisurely, she dried them with a towel, inserting a finger between his big toe and the one next to it. Ah, he liked that. He jerked forward, locking her finger with his toes.

He stood up so suddenly, she would have fallen on her backside if he hadn't grabbed her under her arms. There was masculine laughter from those gathered close by as he jerked the tent flap open and unceremoniously hauled her into their temporary home.

So the groom was impatient for his bride after all.

A most auspicious beginning, murmured the *imam* to Hashem, who nervously wiped his brow

***

A newly married man had his priorities. John pushed his bride on top of a bed of pillows, straddling her in one swift move. He bent down and kissed her thoroughly. It was either that or yell at her and he didn't want to start their wedding night that way.

God, he'd forgotten how a kiss could be hotter than a desert. And how he could lose

himself in the heat. Her tongue darted into his mouth mischievously, and immediately, every cell in his body responded like fireworks on July Fourth.

He'd gone too long without her, that must be it. Impatiently, he lifted his head, looking for an opening to her garment, his fingers skimming everywhere. This robe thing must be a version of the chastity belt.

"How the hell do you get out of these mummy sheets?" he finally demanded.

"Husband, we have all night," purred the woman under him, her face flushed from his kiss. She had the voice of a seductress, low and full of promises but instead of answering him, she held a finger to her reddened lips and moved to sit up.

John didn't like the way she could make him forget important things, such as safety and privacy. This wasn't the first time either and that was why he stayed the hell away from her. He put his weight on his knees, so she could slide up into a sitting position. He liked that she had to look up at him this way, so he didn't move. Not when he fully intended to be on top tonight. He watched as she removed part of her head covering, loosening her collar and exposing her neck and shoulders. The object dangling from a chain around her neck caught his attention, stopping his more lustful inclinations for an instant. She took the chain off and handed it to him.

"Continue what you're doing," he ordered, before reluctantly getting off her so he could use the micro scanner to search the room for listening devices. Apparently, she didn't trust things to be as they seemed.

She continued taking off her garment slowly, watching him with her tawny whiskey-colored eyes. They could make a man weak in the knees with just a heated look, yet would glitter with predatory alertness when she sensed danger. He dreamed of those eyes often—half-open, slightly tilted at the corners, a dreamy wildness in them just before she succumbed to passion. He would wake up sweaty and horny in the middle of the night, cussing at their agreement.

Her burnished brown hair was longer, braided down well below her shoulders. A gray tank top clung to her, emphasizing her small breasts. Its oval neckline was mouthwateringly low, and when she bent forward to untangle that horrible thing she was wearing, the soft mounds looked like they were going to pour out of the top. John swore softly, and she glanced up, fake innocence in her eyes.

The tent was "clean," and she nodded when he handed her gadget back.

"Missed me?" she asked, stretching out of her clothes.

A fine film of perspiration covered her body, clad only in the taunting tank top and underwear. Clothes were amazing things, John concluded, looking at the concealing garment tossed on the floor and what she had on now. And the woman who wore both had the same effect on him, no matter how many layers she put on. Missed her? That ought to be the understatement of the year. He watched her hungrily. And angrily. She had no right invading his world so unexpectedly.

"What the hell are you doing here?" he asked, pitching his voice to a low growl. "I was supposed to exchange the weapons for the downed pilot—and babe," his eyes swept down her body, "you certainly don't look like the picture of Captain James Kirby to me."

"He's dead."

John sucked in his breath. That wasn't the answer he'd expected. "What do you mean?" he demanded. "They wanted weapons for the hostage. There was no way they were going to kill him till I saw him. I want some explanations, Kel."

"Leiha."

John frowned.

"Leiha," Kel insisted, calmly standing up and looking around the tent. She seemed totally unaware what her half-naked body was doing to him. She opened a small trunk and pulled out a towel. "Your wife, remember?"

'That is another thing I want explained," John said grimly. He walked purposefully to her and put both hands on each of her arms. Damn. He wanted to shake her and pull her close at the same time. "Quit playing games with me, Kel."

Kel's head snapped up, her eyes glittering. "I thought that was what you like, Dallas," she drawled. "When you walked out of my life, I remembered distinctly your last words being, 'I can't leave the game, babe. If you want to get married, catch me by surprise.' I don't know what you're complaining about."

He stared at her. "That was—" He paused. He tended to yell when he was frustrated, but now wasn't the time to lose his cool. Taking a deep breath, he adjusted the volume of his voice. "—three years ago! And you're taking my words out of context. You were after marriage, babe, and you gave me an ultimatum."

"Hah. And like a coward, you left." She pushed against his chest, trying to break free.

Ignoring her efforts, John hauled her closer. "Of all the twisted—! You were the one who walked out on me!"

He'd woken up one morning and she was gone, having left a note telling him where to find her. As if he was going to run after her. So he'd given her time to cool off but, after a while, it became abundantly clear it was over when she wouldn't even take his calls. Not long after that, she'd requested a transfer and she was out of his life. Well, that suited him just fine. He didn't have time to mess around with a smart-mouthed trainee, no matter how addicted he was to her mouth.

God, he *had* missed her. Every day, like a man on narcotic withdrawal. It'd been years, but that kind of high was unforgettable. His training had been his salvation. He'd ruthlessly pushed away that part of him that wanted her back. He had a job to do, lives to save. Time passed quickly when you traveled all over the world negotiating with danger and death.

But now, time seemed meaningless because here she was, in his arms again. That same lush mouth was curled into the mocking pout that make him think of sex. Apparently, he was still a hopeless addict.

And, he still loved her. Wanted her.

"Nonsense. You didn't even call me for a month!" Kel slithered her arms up his chest and locked her fingers behind his neck. "That meant you walked away from me first."

John ignored the way her breasts were pushing against his body. There was an argument going on here. He wouldn't lose just because she was trying to distract him with unfair tactics.

"When you didn't return my calls, that meant you wanted out," he countered. He also tried to ignore the sensuous undulating of her lower body against his. Well, parts of him weren't succeeding. A growing part definitely wasn't. He muttered, "I wasn't going to make a move until you gave in."

It sounded stupid now, whatever murderous revenge he'd planned to take when he saw her again. Incredibly stupid, when he knew he could have been doing all the undulating he wanted with her the last three years. The reasons he'd given her were still valid, though, but he was sure he could have talked her into agreeing with him if he'd been given it chance.

Kel glanced down meaningfully at the part of him that was moving. A mischievous smile lifted her lips. "Food or fight, honey?" she purred, conjuring up naughty images of good times spent in his bed feeding each other strawberries and cream. Naked.

John swallowed a laugh. No one but his Kel was such an outrageous lover. And she always had her mind on food—and sex—a truly hungry woman at all times. He frowned at how easy it was to start thinking of her as his again. No way. Not again.

"Okay, fine, I'll play. So we're here in no man's land between Pakistan and India. Tell me why you chose this place for our honeymoon," he asked. "And where is the dowry? Most importantly, what is it?"

The simple assignment he thought he had, a quick H-A-X—hostage/arms exchange—had more twists and turns than he liked. First, he'd been informed the exchange location had been moved to mountain terrain. Then he'd found out that there was no way two parties could meet in the mountains and not be noticed, and the Resistance insisted on a marriage façade. He had balked, like any man would.

His famous temper started factoring in when a call from HQ instructed they wanted him to go through with it, that the game had changed. The dowry was important, the messenger told him. He had to go along with the marriage. Lives were at stake. Okay, lives were in danger, so he had agreed to it. Things could be undone when the mission was over.

The woman in his arms had all the answers. That meant she had the advantage on him. He didn't like that one bit. Who was in charge of this assignment, anyhow?

"Don't you like it here?" his tormentor questioned, obviously enjoying herself. She'd always liked beating him at anything. "Lord and master. Four wives. All the women you want.

You're in absolute control. Male heaven, I'd imagine."

"So how come I feel absolutely powerless?" John murmured, more to himself than her. He played with her braid, twisting the end of it with his forefinger. "How come I'm the one who feels he's been forced into marriage? I know that was what you wanted from me, babe, but this is an extreme way to get a husband."

She shrugged. "I figured three years were long enough. A woman can only wait so long, Dallas."

"Who said I wanted you to wait?" he taunted, slowly twisting the thick braid around his hand now.

"Wasn't that part of our argument?" she reminded him, unconcerned he had her prisoner by the hair. She mocked him with an imitation of his voice, continuing, "'I think we should wait, Kel. This thing we have could fizzle out, Kel. Let's wait for a few years, Kel.'"

John winced at those quotes. Damn woman had the memory of an elephant. He held her head still as he lowered his. Her eyes gleamed back in the gaslight expectantly. A nasty thought occurred. "You waited three years to make your move?"

Her smug smile answered him better than words. He tightened his hold of her braid as the revelation sunk in. The woman was incredible. She had a move planned years in the future.

Catch me by surprise.

This was a fucking long con.

"Three years? You decided three years ago to get me to marry you? That couldn't be!" He looked at her incredulously.

"Hate to point out the obvious. You are, as of today, married to me."

Murderous. That was what he felt. Yet, he'd also had to admit he hadn't felt quite as alive as he did now for a long, long time. The years without her paled in comparison to her presence in his life. Kel had a way of making every minute memorable. He placed an experimental kiss on her waiting lips, as if tasting them for the first time.

"I'll have to think of my next move to get out of this trap," he said against her lips.

Another thought occurred. "Ha, I'm married to a woman named Leiha, not Kel."

Her smile grew wider. "Technical, technical."

She lifted her lips and kissed him back the same way, softly and tenderly, as if she'd waited for a long time for this moment. Three years, actually, John thought, still in disbelief.

"Husband mine—Leiha is short for Kaleiha, the Muslim dimunitive for Kel. It's allowed in this society to have our names in Arabic."

John wanted to...he never ever knew exactly what he wanted to do with Kel Grant. She'd been a trainee in the program but sometimes he wasn't sure who was training whom. And like a damned fool, he'd chosen to ignore the part of him that screamed not to get involved with a woman like her. Look what that had gotten him into.

His disgust must have shown on his face because Kel laughed, not a bit perturbed her groom should be so reluctant on his wedding night. The combination of her scent and herbal powder was heady enough to make him consider forgetting about winning an argument right now and do what he wanted.

"Come on, Dallas," her smoky voice mocked. "All these years working for the Temple should have taught you something. There's always more than one move."

"Oh?" Not if you were trapped. Checkmate. But he wasn't one to ignore a way out when it was offered.

"It's easy, actually. It's an Arab marriage. All you have to do is say 'I divorce you' three times and you have your freedom back."

But of course. "I knew that," John said.

"See? You can say that any time and we're through."

"Just like that? I can say that now?" he challenged, wanting to push her as much as she was pushing him.

Her gaze turned predatory. "I let you go the last time, didn't I?" she asked softly. "Go on. Say it now if it makes you feel better."

John studied her face as she waited. She looked like a doll—big eyes, delicate nose, elegant arching dark eyebrows, lips made for kissing. But he knew the woman underneath; she was no lightweight in the gray matter area. What was it about her that made things both simple and complicated at the same time? He could say those words now, undo the deed, and that should set the record

15

straight. If he wanted to be married, he'd be the one doing the asking. Three easy words to say. It was his feelings that were causing difficulties.

"Later," he said instead. She wanted out so fast? She could wait.

"Dallas?"

"What now?"

"You going to hang onto my hair all night or are you going to kiss me?"

"Actually, I was going to hang you with your hair." He looked at it, wound around his hand three times. "I can't believe how long it's grown."

She moved even closer against him and he forgot about her hair for the moment.

"Dallas, if you don't kiss me properly, I'm going to tell all the women out there tomorrow you're a lousy lover."

"I want it on record I'm doing this under duress," he informed her as he lowered his head to her uplifted face.

"Duly noted. Now kiss me like a lover should. You're out of practice."

A man could only take so many insults. John decided to show her being married meant she could be shut up, just like that. Her mouth opened eagerly under his, and he started practicing.

***

Kel Grant loved two things in her life. Her job and her man. One she kept a secret, the other she kept an eye on. She'd never known a life other than this one and sometimes, she felt some regret she couldn't lead a normal existence, one with a nine-to-five job and a husband and two kids. But she found out you couldn't just to be something other than what she was, the child of two treasure hunters who doubled as spies. Normal life? What was that?

She was a highly-trained strategist. And power was the game that all powerful people played. She was part of that game, and she enjoyed it immensely. Partly because she was well-paid for it, and partly because it, in turn, rewarded her as no nine-to-five job could.

That John Dallas was the love of her life was a secret even to those in her inner circle.

There must be no vulnerable chink in her armor if she were to do her job right. She had asked him one time, and one time only, to get out of the game. When he'd refused, she knew she had to let him go for a while. A close call with death right after that convinced her she'd done the right thing. John Dallas could end up a target if anyone knew how important he was to her. The long hours of recuperating alone in her room gave her time to do what she did best—to think, to lay out a strategy of defense.

How did you keep a love safe? A clean break. How would you keep an eye on love? Be in power. How could she go on living without her love? Commit to a time-schedule to get him back. What if he wouldn't take her back by then? Worse, what if he found somebody new by then? She was a master strategist; she'd deal with those problems when they arose. Lately, she'd been hearing things about the Black Knight. He'd been asking questions about certain classified assignments and she'd felt the ripples of concern from those who didn't like to be questioned. Her sources were good. Her love, she was told, could be in danger from all sides, and no one would help him then.

Well, she had kept an eye on him all along, hadn't she? Time to come in and...and what?

She had a game plan but it was not easy to manipulate John Dallas. He was one of the Temple's best operatives, specializing in hostile negotiations. The man's instincts were fine-tuned to every invisible signal given on both sides of a bargaining table; he would be suspicious of any obstacles that appeared to be out of place.

In fact, she knew there was no way to stop his persistence. He'd try to get answers. But if she were close by, at least she would know when he was too near the truth for his own good. One thing was eminently clear—only she could protect him. She didn't trust anyone else not to sacrifice him for the sake of the game.

Three years hadn't diminished two facts. She still loved him to pieces. And he still sent her up in flames with just his kiss. No one kissed like John Dallas. Slow and wet and sensuous. Searching and finding all the secret dreams of her soul, as he sucked on her tongue and explored every part of her mouth. Releasing her lips, only to recapture them, until there was no doubt who owned them.

Mine, he told her silently, as he ate her like a sumptuous feast. *Mine*, he demanded, as he drank and sipped as if she were his favorite '84 Merlot. Mine, he claimed, over and over again, his tongue dancing with hers in an endless promise.

How, she wondered in a daze, in between his kisses, had she survived this long without him? She moaned softly as he sank deeper into her, trapping her under his weight. When John finally lifted his lips from hers, Kel found herself looking into his fierce dark eyes. This close, she could see the light gray ring around the black orbs, with the luminous gray striations that had always fascinated her. When he was angry, they seemed to flash like tiny lightning bolts. As they were doing right now.

Kel grinned up at him. She liked her opponents angry, that is, as long as she remained calm. His black brows crinkled together in suspicion.

"You know I want you," he stated the obvious, since she could feel just how much he did, "and I have questions that go beyond this job. Hell, it might take me another three years to get all my questions answered, but this isn't the time and place. Kel, what are you doing here?"

"And if I tell, what then?" she baited.

He shifted position, putting more weight on his elbows, glaring furiously as her smile grew ever wider. "Damn your kinky ass, you always liked to get me up at the wrong times." He leaned down closer, as if to kiss her again, then shook off the temptation. "What is your role in the game, Kel?

This time, his voice brooked no argument. She lifted a hand to stroke his thick hair back. It was a little damp from the heat and perspiration.

"I was in the vicinity when the Sphinx went down," she explained, "and they sent word to retrieve some information from the surviving pilot. Being a woman, I had to move among the villagers but the Resistance was very helpful, craftier than we'd thought. They have a smuggling system that is quite sophisticated, using the villagers, especially the women. You would be amazed how many places you can hide weapons under that black garment."

John's eyes lit up with interest. Kel knew he liked this kind of information for future negotiation ventures.

"Continue," he said.

"Don't you want to get more comfortable?" she invited. "You must be hot in those clothes."

"Very," he admitted, "but I like being on top of you too much. I missed this, you know."

Her heart bloomed with pleasure. She had wondered whether he still wanted her as much as she wanted him. Time was different for a man and she was too realistic a woman to imagine John's feelings had remained constant.

"I missed this too," she told him softly.

The flecks in his dark eyes gleamed. "But not enough, apparently." There was a hint of bitterness in his voice. As if he didn't want to think about it, he changed the subject back. "Go on. Tell me what happened to the pilot. I was set to do the H-A-X and now you tell me the Resistance knocked him off. What did he have on him anyway?"

"I didn't say they killed him. He was in worse shape than anyone let on, and was already dying when I got to him. On the way down he landed in a ravine that cut up his chute." Kel lost her playful mood for the moment as she recalled the dead man. "The villagers really couldn't do anything about his head injury."

"What about the Sphinx?"

"You know the government's men are swarming over the thing by now, trying to dismantle it. Study everything."

"I don't get it," John said. "Why then are we exchanging arms for a dead man? The Temple was very specific. Their instructions was to keep the Sphinx's technology out of non-US hands. That makes it pretty clear that the client are the US government this time."

Kel watched as he mulled the information over in his mind. His weight left hers as he turned on his back to lie at her side. He stared up at the ceiling, continuing to ask questions, his voice quieter now. She didn't attempt to answer him, understanding he was just thinking out loud. That he was doing so told her a lot about how much he trusted her and she felt a little twinge of discomfort at her trickery. She firmly tucked it away. Keeping him safe at all cost was all that mattered.

"Why does the Temple care about the Resistance? Why aren't we negotiating with those who shot the Sphinx down?" John jerked his head to the side, looking her straight in the eye. "Unless the pilot is the most important thing. What is it, Kel? They must've known I'd arrive too late. What does the dead Captain have that could be more important than the newest military air toy? Who are we negotiating for? What information did you retrieve?"

Kel turned to lie on her side so she could see him better. His flowing robe hid most of his body from her eyes, but it also emphasized the breadth of his shoulders. He never did like wearing too many layers, so it was easy to guess he hated what he had on. Her John was essentially a T-shirt and jeans man, but sometimes casual clothing wasn't an option in his job as a high-stakes negotiator.

"Relax. Take off your clothes," she ordered softly. Well, she had her own selfish reasons.

This time, it was his turn to smile at her. A sinfully wicked curve of those sexy lips. It sent shivers down her back, and it was way too hot to catch a chill. Always a tough negotiator, he asked, "And what would I get in return?"

She rested her head on her arm. "What do you want?" she teased, ever the strategist. "Me? Or answers to your questions?"

He didn't even take a moment to consider. "You."

"That's nice," Kel murmured, and pulled at the cloth covering his neck, "but why do I get the feeling you'll try to get the answers anyway, likely using unfair methods?"

His smile became even more wicked, if that was possible, as he began to loosen the top of his garment from the thick waistband. His eyes never left her as his hands tugged at his clothes. "Oh, it'll be very fair," he promised. "You'll find it extremely satisfying."

Kel's breath caught as his naked chest came into view. Lord, but the man had a nice chest—smooth where it should be, lightly patterned with hair where needed. She was suddenly greedy to see more, but he was deliberately moving too slowly. With rare impatience, she ripped off the loosened sash at his narrow waist, along with a bunch of buttons. She didn't notice John had become still, passively letting her do as she wanted. She didn't notice anything at all, in fact, but the tremendous swell straining against his white underwear.

"Oh my," she whispered. And licked her lower lip. She ignored John's choked groan. When she reached out her hand, he grabbed it.

"I thought you wanted me out of my clothes," he reminded her, although his voice sounded a little forced.

Kel had waited all this time; she could wait another five minutes. Besides, she had her reasons to prolong this little torture. It wasn't easy, but she swallowed her impatience.

"Okay," she said.

John literally slid out of his clothes, not even sitting up to remove his pants. He kept his eyes on her as he kicked them out of the way. She took in all of him—the thickly muscled arms, the flat stomach, the powerful thighs covered with a fine sheen of perspiration. The years had made him leaner.

There was one offending garment left. She stared at the item meaningfully.

"What do you want?" John echoed her earlier question.

Kel reluctantly looked up and the desire smoldering in his dark eyes was almost too much. But things were moving faster than she wanted. She wanted to make sure that the information she'd be giving John Dallas tonight was just the right amount, no more, no less. If her timing was off, she knew he'd force her to answer the questions she didn't want to. Exactly what happened three years ago.

She inched a little closer, taking great delight in being so close to her man again, taking in everything she had missed so much—his scent, his nonchalant sexuality, his responsive body—and wanting more than anything else to close the emotional gap between them.

"Food," she replied, and it wasn't exactly a lie. "I haven't eaten since midday."

***

John stared back at Kel. She was serious. She really meant food. He didn't doubt it because he knew how ridiculous her metabolism was. The woman could out-eat a horse.

"You teased me out of my clothes and now you want to eat?" he asked. He slowly turned until they were facing each other, several inches apart. "What sort of wifely behavior is that?"

"You did ask me what I wanted." She looked at him in amusement. "Dallas, you just have to learn how to slow down a bit. Besides, you always did like to watch me eat."

John laughed huskily. "You're the only woman I know who thinks food is foreplay." He leaned forward and kissed her. "You're going to have to hurry. This husband is hungry too."

He needed to calm his raging libido, anyway. There were things more important than sex. *Yeah, keep telling yourself that, John, while your brain cells and important body parts vehemently object.* Kel Grant didn't just show up like a desert mirage for no reason; the woman had specifically avoided being physically near him for years. Sure they had one or two conversations on the phone whenever their jobs happened to cross paths, and she'd never hidden the fact that she still found him attractive, but no matter how hard he tried to persuade her, she'd never once agreed to see him.

Not once. Until now.

He wasn't given the codename Black Knight for nothing. The moniker wasn't meant to denote some romantic notion of a medieval warrior—his name came from the chess piece. In the game—as this covert group of underground treasure hunters called it--the Knight negotiated a stealthy path, neither straight nor diagonal, hiding motive and purpose from his opponents. He was trained to see what others hid, and Kel Grant, the woman who had haunted him all this time, was hiding a lot.

Part of him accepted that because she was an operative doing her job. Part of him was furious because she'd chosen to play his opponent instead of his sidekick. Every move she'd made so far was a delay tactic. He was, after all, a negotiator in this business, and she was nowhere near capable of hiding anything from him for long.

His eyes narrowed as he watched her walk to the tent's back entrance. She bent forward to pick up a large tray that he hadn't noticed before, giving him a tempting view of those bikini briefs that barely covered her ass.

Yeah, some negotiator, Dallas. So far, his wonted steel-trap mind and cool logic had failed to function at all. Things that he'd been trained not to allow to influence him had dominated all the present negotiation—a low cut wisp of a tank top, a pair of long legs he knew were ballerina-flexible. Her tempting mouth. He frowned. How many others had kissed her since they parted?

He angrily jerked up into a sitting position. Let her eat. Let her relax. It'd give him a chance to settle down so he could concentrate on other matters, like getting information about this operation. What she'd told him so far had only led to more questions.

Kel was a courier, not a negotiator, so she had information to pass on, obviously retrieved from that dead pilot. But to whom was she passing it on? And what could be so important that the Temple sent her ahead of him? They apparently had suspected the pilot might not survive.

That didn't surprise him. The Temple seldom executed any plan without a dozen moves thought out ahead; he was, after all, part of that system, and understood very well the strategic lessons of preparation.

However, things had gone through too many unexpected twists lately, and the pattern pointed not to coincidence, but to planning. He studied the woman laying out the small plates of food on the eating mat. How much did she know? Or was she just on a routine courier mission?

At that instant, Kel turned around, her head cocked. "Well, are you going to eat with me, or not?" Dressed as she was, she looked slightly ridiculous sitting on the ground, in the traditionally demure female position, feet tucked sideways. And her smile was anything but demure. "Aren't you hungry?"

John felt his body responding to her unspoken invitation. There was no way he could hide how she affected him, not when he was down to his underwear. He joined her on the mat with a grimace. Cross-legged wasn't one of his favorite positions.

He looked into her amused eyes, and the conflicting emotions rose in him again. He wasn't pleased to see her; he was ecstatic to see her. He didn't want her around; he wanted her to stay. He needed to question her about the operation; he was dying to talk about the two of them.

He glanced quickly at his watch. Daybreak was his deadline. Accepting a bowl of roasted meat from her, he smiled. "Sure." Wanting to test her, he continued, "After we eat, I'd like to be entertained with some stories, Scheherazade."

Kel paused with the food halfway between her bowl and mouth, and then he was rewarded with a rich, husky laugh. And, like the newly married queen from A Thousand and One Nights, the woman in front of him settled back, looking absolutely confident she could keep her husband interested all night long.

John Dallas couldn't take his eyes off her. He was hungry all right. But not for food.

Enveloping Attack. *An attack from behind the enemy forces.*

Counter play. *The opposite side takes aggressive action. A player who has counterplayed well puts himself on equal footing with his opponent.*

CHAPTER TWO

John closed his eyes, relinquishing all control. Her hands touched him. Her lips. Her mouth. Her tongue took over his world, which had rapidly diminished into one burning powerful need as he had somehow ended up on his back after dinner. She explored his body, first with her small hands, gliding all over each part of him so slowly he had to grit his teeth to stop from begging. Her hair was the softest silk—he couldn't remember undoing that braid—as she bent her head. His muscles tightened wherever he felt her lips following the path of her hands, a sensuous, wet path that stopped to investigate all the right spots. She sucked his nipples, nibbled her way down his stomach...damn if the woman wasn't hungry still...and he groaned as her mouth hovered over his painfully erect cock.

Take it. Take me. Was he even speaking in English? He couldn't hear himself amid the roar in his ears. He was so hot for her, he was going to...and then her lips closed around him and he groaned. He was in heaven. And she was the angel of his dreams returned to him. She rolled her tongue and he almost shot off the floor in response. The welcome wetness of her mouth took...everything.

Everything. When she'd left him, he felt she'd taken everything with her, but he could never name what those things were. It was just the emptiness inside that told him she took something valuable.

She caressed her balls as her tongue tortured the whole length of him over and over. He pushed up, wanting to go deeper in her mouth, but the slight squeeze of her hand controlled his eagerness. Her teeth lightly punished him and then her tongue returned, paying extra attention to the underside of his penis, where he was the most sensitive. *She remembered.* And he was helpless to the growing pleasure enveloping his senses.

A growl escaped his lips in protest when she stopped. *Don't. Stop.* She only laughed and came back up to kiss him. God, she tasted so good. He pushed his tongue into her mouth with the ravenousness of a wild man. How many others had there been? The surge of jealousy caused him to kiss her more roughly than he intended, but he didn't care any more. She was his wife, wasn't she? She was his.

His. He lifted her off him and was on her immediately. Flesh on flesh. He was going to take back what was his. How dare she leave him?

Her throaty encouragement urged him on as she moved sinuously under him. He didn't need her to tell him what she wanted—he could feel her wet and ready.

"John."

How could the mere whisper of his name in his ear make him almost lose his control? It was the way she said it. She never called him John, except during heated moments of intimacy. John—in that husky murmur. John—almost French sounding, the way she sighed it out. She gripped his arms as he guided himself inside her.

Hot. She clenched around him in fierce possession, all sleek feminine eagerness. He pushed and almost lost it again when she arched into him with wild abandon. Stroke for stroke, she drove him higher and higher.

He tried to focus. Her eyes were half-closed, looking back at him. Little pants escaped her parted lips. He couldn't really see. Or think.

He slowed his thrusts, moving deep inside her and sliding out, wanting more from her. He reached down between them, reaching for her wetness, searching. She gasped. *Ah yes. More, Kel. Wife. More.* He rubbed her as he continued his slow ride. Her hands were suddenly holding his buttocks, trying to set a faster pace, but he didn't relent. Thrust down hard, thumb circling her little clitoris as he slowly pulled out, thrust down hard, repeat as she got wetter and wetter, as her breaths became harder. It excited him to hear her throaty whispers, begging him to go a quicker. He bent down and nibbled her neck, breathing in her unique scent. She groaned louder, and he realized the new position put more weight where he was intimately massaging her. He smiled and as her fingers dug deeper into his flesh, his finger stroked her a little harder, even as he ground deeper into her sweet heat.

"John...john...johhhnn!"

Forget focus. His world exploded into pure heat. And still he kept driving into her, needing her all over again. Her writhing response only rekindled the pleasure that washed his senses in waves.

Sated, John closed his eyes.

***

When he reopened them, everything still looked out of focus. He frowned. His body was stiff, as if he had been sleeping in the same position too long. As the ceiling of the tent became clearer, so did his thoughts.

What time was it? His wrist appeared in front of his eyes and the watch read 0600 hours. Six in the morning? He squinted. He couldn't remember going to bed. Couldn't remember a damn thing after he sat down to eat dinner with Kel.

He jerked up as if hit by an electrical current. Images swam in his mind—images way too sexy to be just a dream. He looked down. Oh yeah, he was naked under the sheet over his body. The pillow next to him had an indentation. Her scent lingered tantalizingly on him still.

Something was very wrong. He usually didn't have sensational sex and not remember doing it. Well, actually he recalled some pretty incredible details, but the memory felt...distant.

A cough interrupted his disarrayed thoughts, and John looked in its direction, ready to demand an explanation.

Except that the woman sitting quietly near the entrance to the tent wasn't Kel. It was the other one of the woman who had sat beside her in the donkey cart yesterday.

What the hell was going on? John's eyes caught sight of the previous night's leftovers sitting innocently on the tray not too far away. A nasty suspicion surfaced. Fury awoke the rest of his half-asleep mind.

"She told me to tell you not to yell," the stranger in his bridal tent softly said, her accented voice trembling slightly from fear. "She said shouting would only make trouble."

John glared at the woman, even though it wasn't her fault he was wearing only his birthday suit in a stuffy tent in the mountains of goat-herding country. And oh yeah, he was the top-notch liaison who was supposed to be in charge of a hostage arms exchange. At current status, he had no hostage and had given away a whole cache of arms.

He scowled fiercely, although cussing would have felt better. A strange woman was less than ten feet away from his naked ass, and she was already looking at him as if he were an ogre.

"Where is she?" he asked, his morning voice huskier than usual.

He cleared his throat and looked around the tent to make sure Kel wasn't hiding under any of the camel-hair sheets. The other woman's gasp halted his scan, and looking down he noticed the not-too-big coverlet protecting what was left of his modesty had moved and now he was really in danger of scaring the poor lady. She was, after all, bundled up like a proper religious woman, and he had no idea whether she was for real or not. Her horrified eyes seemed to say she was definitely for real, though.

John sighed, and pulled the sheet higher. Ooops. Too high, judging from her ever-widening eyes. He tugged at the other end of the sheet. Obviously, his wife thought this up as some final joke. His wife. He glared at the woman again, and repeated his question. "Where's Leiha?"

To his relief, the woman took her eyes off his body, and answered, "I am Leiha."

Oh, that was all he needed. Morning-after surprises. "I mean Leiha, my wife." He tried to sound reasonably patient. He could have been crude by explaining about the Leiha who had been naked beside him the night before, but he had a feeling that would only earn him more female problems.

"For now, I am Leiha, your wife." She stepped closer, in the manner of a person approaching an angry bear.

That was it. John's patience was definitely wearing thinner by the second. He moved forward and she shrieked, falling back a few steps. "Leiha, or whoever you are," he told her, wondering whether he had somehow woken up in the twilight zone, "I just want my clothes. Okay? Look, they're all over the place. If you can just throw me...ummm (skip the underwear, he decided)...the pants over there, I'd really appreciate it."

She vigorously nodded her head in agreement, and ran to fetch the garment. Staying a few feet away, she tossed the trousers into his arms.

John waited. And waited. Finally, he sighed. "If you don't turn around, I can't put them on without embarrassing you."

It mustn't have occurred to her, for her face went fiery red. But she still didn't turn away.

"I have never seen a naked man before," she told him.

29

Oh, now he was the zoo animal for display. "Lady, I'm sorry to hear that, but until we've been properly introduced, I'd rather not give lessons in anatomy, if you don't mind."

He watched in amusement as she finally turned her back with a show of reluctance.

A few minutes later, he was dressed enough to conduct a normal conversation, although there was nothing normal about the whole damned state of affairs. It was barely six-thirty in the morning, and he felt as if time had escaped him somehow.

Leiha, the other Leiha, *his* Leiha, was still missing. This new one was moving around the tent as if she were really his wife, picking up discarded clothes and putting things away in the small trunks by the entrance. He scratched the back of his neck in frustrated disbelief.

"What else did she say, besides not to shout?"

The woman dug into her robes, and pulled out a piece of paper. "She wrote you this letter."

John tore the envelope quickly.

Dallas, I know you'll remember everything I told you last night. This is Zaleiha, your wife, for now. Treat her like a regular H-A-X. Take her with you and hand her over at your next stop. She can't return to the village now because she is, of course, me, and you and your wife's journey will be watched over. I'm sorry I couldn't stay with you, but Leiha must get out of the village as part of the agreement. I know how much your freedom means. If you like, I'll mutter 'I divorce you' three times as soon as I cross the border, once you've completed your assignment. Be careful.

Love, Kel

P/S Eat this note when you've memorized the deets.

P/P/S Last night was more than fair. Let's do this info barter again some time.

John wanted to pull his hair out. He'd barely been with Kel for twenty-four hours and already she was driving him crazy. The trouble with her was, he never knew what was going on in her head. She was one complicated package, always with her fingers in ten different projects. She was the only woman who made him want to strangle and kiss her all at once.

I know how much your freedom means. He squashed the note, startling Kaleiha, who was watching him with fear in her eyes again. Just to appease his current bad mood, he scowled at her fiercely and, just like that, the woman dropped the folded garments in her arms and scuttled off heading for the tent exit.

Ah, shit. John sighed, attempting to control his temper. "Don't be frightened," he said. "You're Zaleiha, right?"

She nodded. "She said you were going to be like a drunk donkey when you woke up," she said, her voice accusing, "and that I've to get you a cup of coffee with lots of milk."

"Donkeys don't get drunk," John pointed out politely, as he found his underwear and stuffed them into one of his pockets. He spied the sash for his robe and went to retrieve it. "But yes, coffee with milk. That sounds like the best thing right now."

As if she had been waiting for his permission, Zaleiha immediately went over to a tray and poured coffee out of a flask. The aromatic brew must be strong as hell because the whole tent smelled of roasted coffee immediately. John took a deep breath, wondering if that might just kickstart his brain cells again.

He accepted the cup from her, looking at the coffee longingly. "You didn't spike this too, did you?"

"Spike?" She frowned.

"Spiked...as in drugged."

"Oh." She nodded in comprehension, then, realizing she might be misunderstood, quickly shook her head. "Of course not. She says you'll kill her if your coffee doesn't taste right." She cocked her head. "You must be a very nasty-tempered man, killing so easily."

Did she just make a joke? John sipped on his coffee, studying the woman. She had a very earnest demeanor, when she wasn't cowering. "Well, bad coffee is a serious

31

offense," he commented, and took another big gulp. "But not to worry, this particular batch is absolutely fine."

"She made it herself."

John sighed. Might have known. "Is there anything else she said to you?"

It pissed him off, having been out-maneuvered like that. He knew the Temple was behind it, but why did it have to be Kel? If it'd been anyone else, he wouldn't have been so easily tricked. He was pretty sure the sex was just Kel's own way to poke a little fun at him. Okay, so it'd been fun for him too, but surely she knew she didn't need to drug him for that kind of cooperation? He'd have been more than willing.

"She said lots of things, but I don't know which parts were meant for your ears."

John looked at Zaleiha, who resumed putting away things. "Where did you learn your English anyway?" he asked. He rolled up the eating mat after she put the dinner trays into a basket.

"We girls all went to school, you know, until the revolution. Now they no longer allow us to be educated. I was going to go to college but my parents were killed." Zaleiha shrugged. "But this is my way out. You are my way out."

For the first time since waking up, John felt in control. Negotiations and exchanges. That was his domain. Zaleiha was part of the H-A-X. "Can you tell me about the pilot that died? The one Kel...my Kaleiha talked to. How did your people find him?"

"The villagers saw the plane come down. Then they found him in a deep...how do you call it...valley? Deep valley?"

"Ravine," John supplied.

"Ravine. Then they kept him for the Resistance. She showed up not long after. I think she talked to the pilot but I'm not sure."

Kel had told him she did. "So the Resistance didn't know the man was dying until they saw him, right?"

She nodded.

"Then Kaleiha showed up and talked to the Resistance and, somehow, you became involved."

"I was chosen because I can speak good English and I'm not married. It's hard to get married when you're smarter than all the men in the village."

John had to smile. He liked the woman's directness. "Right. So you get to come with me, then. Did Kaleiha tell you what's going to happen? Did she prepare you for the journey?"

She gave him an indignant look. "Of course. She was very nice to me and we brokered a deal."

He cocked a brow. This he wanted to hear. "Oh?"

"If she chose me as the one to go to freedom, I've to treat you exactly the way she teaches me."

John crossed his arms. He wished this wondrous teacher was around at the moment. There were several great ways to treat runaway wives in this culture. "And how are you supposed to treat me?"

Zaleiha backed away, her eyes wary. "Very carefully."

***

Two hours later, John felt imminently better. He had freshened up by the river, taking in the banter of the other men in the camp.

Up so early already?

The mountain air wears one out, you know.

Can he make it down the mountain, you think?

He wondered what they would have done if they had woken up to find another woman in their tent.

They were all packed and ready to make their way down the mountain trail. Hashem was the only one in his group who knew the woman on the donkey cart, completely veiled now from head to foot, was not the same woman he had married.

The leader of the visiting group, Ahmin, had a twinkle in his eye when he shook hands with his new 'brother.' "I trust you are pleased with your woman."

John lifted a brow sardonically. "I don't have any complaints."

"We are happy too. We needed the supplies you gave us."

They climbed onto their horses, trotting side-by-side with him for part of the way to show respect. John studied Ahmin, who looked like a regular tribesman until he spoke in that New York accent. He wore an expensive wristwatch and gave the impression of being well-traveled, answering a few questions about other parts of the United States with a small smile, as if he knew he was being probed. John wondered at the circumstances that made an obviously Westernized, educated man decide to go to war. But it was none of his business. His job had always been only as the go-between, making sensitive, unsavory exchanges governments didn't wish to be publicly known.

Lately, however, he had some questions he knew could get him into trouble. Little things about the last four or five operations had bothered him. Like this one. With the dead pilot and the obvious fact that an expensive wreckage lay abandoned in these mountains but wasn't, somehow, considered important. That was too weird. Technology like the new Sphinx would make for some serious exchange-negotiations. So, how come the Temple still wanted to extract a dying pilot? And when they couldn't, why did they send a courier? And to retrieve what?

As if reading his mind, the other man turned to him and said, in a low tone, "She is something special. If she weren't so old, I'd have married her myself. She refused, though. She's a tough negotiator. Wanted more than farm animals. She told me she intended to see the Taj Mahal. I hope you can afford such a wife." Again, rich amusement rumbled through his voice, as if he was in on some secret.

John gave a slow smile. A test was a test, after all. The man wanted to see exactly how much John knew about the dead pilot situation. Kel didn't really leave him totally in the dark; they did talk some during dinner.

"We Westerners have something called a honeymoon. She mentioned Agra last night."

"So, we may meet again."

Interesting. Had Kel set a date to meet up with this man? John shrugged. "If it's important enough, I'll be there," he replied.

"Good-bye, then, John Dallas," Ahmin said. "I do miss the United States, you know. New York pizza, nothing like it. And, of course, meeting with married women is unheard of here. I look forward to doing business with your wife. She promised me a good pizza dinner."

John cocked his head. "In Agra? There isn't any real New York pizza there."

Ahmin gave a soft laugh. "I'm sure she'll tell me the next time I see her."

A message. Kel was going to pass on more than food between this man and someone in Agra. And maybe elsewhere. How many times had Ahmin and Kel met? Damn it, how well did they know each other?

They parted company, moving in opposite directions. It killed John not to be able to pull the man off his horse to ask him exactly when and how he was meeting Kel Grant. Kel Dallas, he corrected grimly. Oh, the journey downhill would provide ample time for him to think out a plan.

First, he would reassemble all the information Kel had given him last night. Then he would piece it together with what he'd found out through Zaleiha and Ahmin. Lastly, he was going to give his wife a hell of a surprise.

Pizza dinner, right?

Would she really mutter "I divorce you" three times like she claimed in the letter? John gripped his horse's reins tightly as he motioned for the men to start moving out. Did she think she could just up and walk away like she did all those years ago? Did she think he'd be satisfied with a quickie Arab divorce, especially now he had her in his arms again? What was he, some sort of a one-night stand before heading off to a date with a pizza-loving, gun-toting, New York tribal lord?

The more he thought about that last question, the more incensed he became. He needed the information she'd retrieved. There was something going down at the

Temple and he intended to find out what. It was important enough to draw Kel out to see him again. His eyes narrowed. Unless, of course, that move was just meant to distract him.

So many missing pieces. He hated it. He wanted to know everything about Kel Grant...Kel Dallas, he muttered under his breath. She wasn't divorcing him until he was damn well ready.

***

It wasn't easy leaving her warm sleeping man in bed. Kel closed her eyes, picturing John asleep, one arm flung over his head, the other holding her hand as if taking her for a walk in his dreams. His mouth had been slightly open, and she'd placed a soft kiss on his lips before leaving.

A night of loving had left her wanting more and her heart screamed at the unfairness of it all. She sighed. What heart? She'd already left it with John Dallas a long time ago, little did the stubborn man know. In many ways he was still the same man she left—damned good at figuring people out; lousy when it came to dissecting his own emotions. Somehow, she confused him. She could see it in the way he constantly fought himself. As an opponent, she could take advantage of this so easily, but as the woman who loved him, she wanted him to be very sure about her. She certainly didn't want him to think she forced him into anything. It wasn't her way.

Of course, she imagined at that moment he probably wasn't confused at all. In fact, he was probably trying very hard not to roar like an injured bear. Poor baby. Kel grinned. He was always such a sore loser. The mild sedative she gave him was just enough to stop his determination to ask too many questions. His motor skills, she recalled in amusement, were functioning just fine. Eyes closed, she crossed her legs as heated images of their time together flooded her mind.

Peeling the underwear from her half-inebriated man was the most erotic thing she'd done in a long time. John

Dallas totally in her power. Oh my. And totally responsive, calling her name in that demanding tone, even with his brain addled. *Take me, Kel,* he'd whispered. Her heart thrilled at those words.

Every inch of his magnificent body was committed to memory. She'd touched him.

Stroked him. Kissed him. Tasted him. And he'd done the same to her.

She quivered as if his hands were caressing her again. The way they moved up her inner thighs. The way he massaged the sensitive area at the top. Then his thumbs moved inward and parted her like a curtain. The growl he gave had her near orgasm, and when he touched her, she'd almost screamed.

He'd explored her like a blind man, slowly and deliberately. Well, the drug gave the effect of pleasant drunkenness, so he probably hadn't been able to focus. Which was what she wanted, she thought, opening her eyes at last. She hadn't wanted him to see too closely, otherwise he'd question things—like her tattoo. She'd just wanted him to touch her.

Damn, she didn't want to think about that right now. She was lonely and missed Dallas.

She hadn't allowed herself to indulge in Dallas-fantasies too often. It made the loneliness even worse afterwards. But this memory was so good. The man was definitely talented in bed, even half-conscious.

She frowned at the twinge of guilt again. Oh, stop. He wouldn't have let her leave on her own and Kel was glad to be away from the traditional confines of the mountain people. To pretend to be subservient 24/7 was no easy feat. She was used to working alone but that wasn't possible in a culture that disapproved of their women getting attention of any kind. In some ways, it'd worked to her advantage; she could move among men without being noticed. Who would have suspected a woman courier? So after the Sphinx's crash she'd managed to slip past the guards and those who patrolled the villages.

John wouldn't have understood. And he'd have definitely insisted on knowing why his presence was needed at all, when the pilot was already dead. His guess that the pilot's message was more important than the aircraft was too close to the truth. Her instructions from HQ had been specific. The message was only for the King's ears. Nobody else.

Once she'd reached the meeting point, changed clothes, and flew across the border to New Delhi, India, she was back in the hustle and bustle of Asian culture, with its open markets and noisy, haphazard traffic, the intense mix of modern industry and ancient temples. Here, after a quick conversation with HQ through a secured line, she became a tourist, constantly hounded by beggars when she ventured out onto the streets.

In this heat, at least, there was air-conditioning in the hotels. And she was glad to have escaped the suffocating head-to-foot burqa. And yes, there was food. Her burp was loud and unladylike as she leaned back from the room service trolley. God, it was wonderful to eat good food again. She had been constantly hungry up in the mountains, restricted by custom and the constant company of other women. The power bars she'd hidden in the folds of her garment tasted like sweaty cardboard after a while. She made a face at the memory.

Indian food had her vote for sure. She looked at the dishes before her. Biryani rice with chicken. Kebabs. Beef baked in clay pots. A culture could be studied by the food its people ate—she popped a piece of the kebab into her mouth—and Indian culture was unapologetically spicy and overdone. She liked it.

The hum of the fax machine by her bed caught her attention, and wiping her hands on the tablecloth, she stood up to check the message. Her new instructions.

She read it twice. Interesting. She'd thought it was going to be a simple meeting with Ahmin in Agra, the historic city, four hours away. That was another thing John wouldn't understand, she thought. The fact that she was meeting the man again after the exchange. Ahmin wanted an audience with the person in charge of this H-A-X. He, like so many in her business, was more than he seemed. In real life, Ahmin was a commando of a top secret US outfit at Command Center, and he certainly knew how to use his very diverse bloodline for his own interests. The few times she'd dealt with him, she'd found him a man very different from the one he portrayed while with "his" people.

Kel scratched her nose as she contemplated the coming meeting. She had a feeling many things were going to happen in Agra. She'd better figure out how to handle them all.

***

"You look different in T-shirt and jeans," Zaleiha commented.

John looked up from the file he was studying. After several dusty days down the mountain trail, they'd finally reached their destination, where they were given papers and changes of clothes. It was the usual drill—bribes, phone calls, more bribes at the checkpoint, and the liaison at the waiting place—but for Zaleiha, it'd been an eye-opener. She'd pulled a dress out of the small suitcase that had been given to her and held it up to her body, exclaiming at how clever Kel was to know the correct size. Then, she'd taken a look at slender pumps included in the case and had fallen in love.

John grinned at the memory. It was funny watching a woman drool over footwear. He'd seen Kel with the same look in her eyes when she shopped for shoes, so he recognized the reaction immediately. Women and shoes. He shook his head. Why there must be three pairs for each outfit was a mystery to him.

"You look different too," he told Zaleiha, who stood at the door of the office. Without those confining clothes, he saw that she was thinner than he'd thought. Her dark hair was traditionally pulled back under a scarf. Her almond-shaped eyes didn't meet his. She was shy, he realized belatedly. He scratched the back of his neck. Hell, he had no knowledge of how to treat shy women. "Umm...come on in. Let me look at you properly."

She obediently walked into the room, carefully placing one foot in front of the other, like a model. "Do you think where I am going, I can buy more shoes?" she asked.

John frowned. "Why, don't you like the three pairs you have?"

"Oh, yes! But Kel said I have to buy another outfit, a nice one, for dinner dates. And I'd need more shoes for that." She bit her lip. "Taller shoes, she said, I think."

"Ah...high heels," John told her, then shook his head in disbelief. He couldn't believe that he'd been assigned the role of professor Higgins to Eliza Doolittle here. High heels and evening gowns, indeed. His frown deepened. "You're not thinking I'll be taking you out to dinner, are you? I won't be around once the next liaison arrives. He or she will take care of you."

"Of course not. You're a married man!" Zaleiha exclaimed in shock. "When I go out to dinner with a man, it will be with an available one. Kel said to look for the right kind."

'Kel said', 'Kel said'. John felt his temper rising again. "Kel seems to have spent a lot of time with you."

Zaleiha nodded. "She asked me many questions, said she wanted to make sure this was the right step for me. She didn't want me to feel out of place, alone and unwanted."

Something glowed inside him, hearing about Kel's concern for a stranger. She very seldom showed this soft side of herself, and he'd forgotten how it made him feel whenever he caught her doing the unexpected things that had nothing to do with The Temple or her job. When he was asked to profile Kel as part of her trainee evaluation, it was the first thing he'd noticed about her. She was very protective of people she cared about.

"Tell me, Zaleiha, how did Kel explain the situation to you? Did you have any idea then who she was and what was happening?"

"Well, I kind of understood some kind of exchange was going to take place. The Resistance likes to do that—trade things with different people. That's how we all survive. Kel told me that she works for a group which specializes in brokering deals between agencies."

Zaleiha frowned, trying to work it out in words. "It's complicated, but she put it in the simplest way, and now I've forgotten how exactly. It has something to do with the war game, checkers."

"Chess," corrected John. "Go on, try to remember exactly how Kel explained it."

"Ummm...something about her job as moving the pieces in the game to make sure the right pieces...the right moves? No, the right pieces...make the right move." Zaleiha shrugged. "I understood it when she said it but not anymore, I'm sorry. She told me about you too, that your job was more active because you were the negotiator, while she is more like a messenger, with special powers."

Kel's explanation was important to John because it told him what she had in mind and how she was playing this particular game. As a negotiator for the Temple, he'd had to set up a dummy corporation as a cover. The parties involved never really knew who they were buying from or exchanging with; usually, they were more than happy with the money and the terms. And if they happened to be inquisitive enough to search deeper, they would just come up with Knights Inc., the dummy front, a company that specialized in treasure hunts. His own group of "knights" were hand-picked by him. He trusted them.

What Kel said to Zaleiha wasn't too far from the truth. He was a negotiator and she was a courier, a messenger. Simple as that. Who they worked for was a little more complicated to clarify. The game wasn't for everyone. Its participants were very selective.

He shuffled through the papers in the folder as he analyzed what he'd found out in the last few days. The thing was, what was he suppose to be negotiating for? And what message did Kel get from the pilot? Usually, all the details were given to him to ensure his success, but lately, it seemed as if someone up there wanted him to fail. This wasn't the first time that he'd conducted business that seemed to have nothing worthwhile in return. He frowned. What was so important about a damned message?

"What are you reading?" Zaleiha interrupted his thoughts.

"Stuff."

"Ahh."

John lifted a brow inquiringly. "Ahh?"

"Kel said—" She stopped when he groaned, lowering his head in a gesture of total defeat. "I'm sorry, is something wrong?"

"No, no, please continue," he said, wanting to hear what other wisdom his Kel had imparted. "What was the "ahhh" for?"

Zaleiha sat down on the Victorian embroidered chair, and crossed and uncrossed her legs, studying how her new shoes looked. Finally, she put them together and tucked her feet femininely to the side

"Kel said," she continued, as she tried to keep her balance, "that 'stuff' means the man doesn't want the woman to know about whatever he's doing. It's part of the secret code of male domination, she said."

John coughed. The woman was incorrigible, and he didn't mean Zaleiha. "I think you shouldn't take Kel so seriously. She has this strange sense of humor that isn't really proper." He could manipulate information just as well as his darling wife.

"She told me to ignore any insults you say about her," Kaleiha informed him, and her eyes widened when she finally looked up from her feet. "Oh, don't be angry. I don't know how to make her good coffee to calm you down...and the other way is impossible."

Okay, he'd bite. "Go on. What is the other way to calm me down? Drug me?" he suggested, with remarkable calm, he might add.

Kaleiha blushed and again, wouldn't look him in the eye. He narrowed his suspiciously.

"Well," she said, her voice shy. "It's impossible because I don't know what to do with a naked man, but Kel said, she can calm you down once you're naked."

John stared at the woman. Her face was bright red with embarrassment. "You know what," he finally said, although the sound of his voice seemed a little choked to him, "I think I'm going to take you to Agra with me. I need to show you off to Kel."

Delight fused with embarrassment. The woman, who, a few days ago, was probably the epitome of a demure and quiet female, jumped up, squealing. She quickly covered her mouth.

"Oh thank you, thank you! Kel said if I said the right things, you would take me along!"

John contemplated tearing the file in his hands in half. Fate giving him one manipulating female was cruel, but to then give him another who was obviously in training to be just as bad was simply evil. He had to go to the source, return this evil thing to the giver. He thought of Kel—he wasn't going to let time pass again. She couldn't hide from him, not ever again. Yes, he was going to find the evil woman in Agra and...and...get naked.

Knight's Tour. *A puzzle or task in which a knight has to move over an empty chessboard, visiting each square only once.*

CHAPTER THREE

"AARRRRRRRGGGGGGGHHHHHH!"

John opened one eye, his right ear ringing from the high-pitched scream. "Take a nap," he advised. "If you don't look, you won't see a damned thing."

The woman beside him sat stiffly, both hands gripping the back rest of the front seat, as she stared with saucer-eyes into the traffic in front of her. In the driver's seat, the turbaned Sikh had one finger poked into his left ear while steering with his thumb pressed insistently on the car horn.

"How can you sleep?" Zaleiha shrieked back over the din. "He is constantly making that horrible sound with the horn! How can you sleep with four hours of car horn?" Her voice rose into a hysterical pitch.

"He needs to do that," explained John in a mild voice, "to let the people ahead of him know he's right on their asses and if they don't move to the other lane, there's going to be a crash."

"That's it! That's it!" Zaleiha yelled. "Why do they drive like there is just one lane? Even I can see there are two lanes clearly marked! Why are the drivers in the middle of the road and why must this driver keep honking until they move? When we used to have television, the people in the shows didn't drive like this!"

John sighed and opened his eyes. It wasn't easy explaining to somebody about driving in a country where no rules was the rule. First of all, there was probably only one traffic light from New Delhi to Agra. One traffic light, and that was near the palatial government building. After that, every citizen for himself, so to speak. Every driver, every school kid on a bicycle, every crammed-to-the-seams busload of Indians, every wagon of workers, every criss-crossing cow for himself. At varying speeds up to eighty miles an hour, he had to admit it could be harrowing to a first timer. He'd learned to just let go of the mounting horror of being killed and take a nap. If that was possible, that is, with everyone beeping their horns as if their life depended on it. Which they did. Just close your eyes, and pretend you're in New York. In the year 2050.

Okay, that was probably not usable advice for a young woman on her first car ride outside a chauffeured slow vehicle. So he patted her on the shoulder in the awkward manner he'd seen his pals use to comfort a crying child.

"It's going to be all right," he said, in what he hoped was a soothing tone of voice. "They're used to it. Really. We are going to arrive in one piece. Right, David?"

David Singh, the Sikh driver, nodded. "Oh yes," he said, shaking his head in typical Indian fashion. "No problem. We're there in no time at all. Maybe five minutes. The Miss has nothing to fear, nothing to be afraid of. I'm a very good driver."

John looked back at Zaleiha. "See? Everything's under control."

At that moment, the car swerved hard to the left, barely missing a wayward cow. Zaleiha's high-pitched scream had both men wincing.

"What control? What control?" she asked, as the car bounced over several packages that fell from the cart ahead. "This is madness! This is a killing field! Why are there cows on the road?"

"They're holy. They can go wherever they want."

"I know they're ho...look out!" She pointed to another cow lumbering toward them, then threw herself against John, hiding her face in his chest as she prayed in her dialect. Her stranglehold on his neck was amazingly strong, and John couldn't disentangle her hands as she sobbed, soaking his T-shirt. He looked up and caught David Singh's sympathetic gaze in the rearview mirror.

John sighed, sinking back into the seat. When they reached Agra, the car would slow down and maybe he could dissuade this woman from making a giant hanky out of him. He'd forgotten exactly why he'd chosen to bring her along...oh yeah, to give her back to Kel. Let her be Professor Higgins.

He forgot about the woman in his arms as soon as they entered the limits of the old city. The head-splitting honking stopped. That was because there wasn't a moving car in sight. Not a soul walking anywhere. It looked like an abandoned town, but with cars parked haphazardly all over the place.

"David?" he asked.

The driver shrugged "We'll reach the hotel in no time at all—no traffic!" He drove on, obviously unperturbed by the non-activity around them.

John frowned. He'd been to Agra before, and at the height of tourism, it was impossible to navigate on foot the closer one traveled to the Taj Mahal. Hawkers roamed everywhere selling fake marble items and bad replicas of the tomb. Beggar children literally chased the unwary foreigner all the way from the hotel to the famous site. And there were the thousands of visitors, locals mingling with the very obvious foreigners, taking photographs and buying mementoes.

Where were they? This was the equivalent of walking down Fifth Avenue all alone. For a moment, he thought that maybe some sort of terrorist virus attack had killed off the population. Then he caught sight of a few cattle strolling down the street. Okay, strike virus-attack off the list.

When they finally arrived at their destination, they found Indian troops in front of the hotel. One of them demanded identification as soon as David Singh rolled down the car window. Hot humid air immediately gushed into the cool interior. David exchanged a few words with the soldier, and then turned to John.

"We aren't allowed to stay here."

John arched a brow. "We have reservations."

"Yes, but the President of the United States has a suite here at the moment. First Lady wants to visit the Taj. Those people in the lounge are all like in the movie Men In Black, you know?"

"Secret Service," John confirmed, as he eyed the black-suited, expressionless men wearing dark sunglasses. Well, at least he now had an explanation as to why the city was deserted. Probably under curfew.

"No one is allowed to move around in the city. Soldier said if you give him some rupees, he will make problem go away."

John sniffed. He doubted it. The Prez's blacksuits weren't going to let an unidentified car slip away without checking him out. "Tell the soldier I'm on my honeymoon, David," he ordered. "And my wife is suffering from the heat."

"Yes, sir."

The soldier looked through the window and studied John, who was still holding Zaleiha.

He shook his head. "Sorry, but security reasons," he said, apologetically. He shook his head sympathetically when Zaleiha moaned into John's chest.

"Look, here are one thousand rupees." John handed over the money. Nothing was going to budge the man until he saw cash and he needed a way to get someone from the Secret Service to talk to him. "My wife really needs some fresh air. If we could just rest up at the restaurant for an hour, then maybe she would feel better. Besides, we aren't allowed to move around the city, so how are we supposed to find other accommodations?"

The soldier pocketed the bill. "You are right, sir. No traveling because of curfew, so you have to at least stay here until I find out what to do."

"Thank you," John said, wryly. He whispered in Zaleiha's ear, "Keep it up."

When the soldier opened the door, John climbed out with Zaleiha in his arms. He took the stairs and walked into the lobby. The Secret Service men spoke to the soldier John had bribed. The one in charge approached.

"How is your wife, Mr....?"

"Dallas. We didn't know about this or we wouldn't have made the four-hour trip from New Delhi, I assure you."

"Why don't you sit down here and we'll get some water for her?" the man said. "I need to ask a few questions, if it's all right. You said you're registered to stay in this hotel. Every guest in this hotel has to be accounted for, and identified. Can I see your reservation papers?"

"No problem," John said. "I understand thoroughly. Can you pull the envelope out of my pocket? My wife is still feeling rather weak. Here, honey, let's just follow this man and sit down in the lobby for a few minutes, okay?"

The man glanced through the papers, then looked up quickly, new respect in his eyes.

"You're John Dallas, CEO of Black Knights, Inc.? Your executive secretary is already here, I believe. A whole suite is reserved for you and there are instructions left with us detailing your arrival. You're late for the Taj Mahal, I'm afraid, but the President and the First Lady are scheduled for another quick tour to Asoka's tomb."

John nodded. No wonder the Secret Service was willing to talk to him; the President wasn't actually in the hotel right now. Interesting how things could change just like that too. He must be getting more important in the Temple's standings, meeting with the President of the United States now. When one didn't know what the hell was going on, the golden rule was to go with the flow.

"Yes, I'm aware of that. My delay was unintentional."

"We'll call up to your suite to announce your arrival. Just pick up the keys at the front desk and go straight up, Mr. Dallas. Sorry that your wife feels so sick."

"She'll be fine." John wondered whether she had fallen asleep, she was so still.

They went to the registration desk and the Secret Service agent gave the papers to the clerk, nodding his approval. "He's on our list. He can come down and sign in later," he instructed. "Let him get Mrs. Dallas upstairs first."

John thanked the man and took the electronic key cards in the small folder. John Dallas. Kel Dallas. His heart skipped a beat. *More and more interesting.*

There was a weapon detection device just outside the elevator. John didn't put Zaleiha down, smiling apologetically at the security guard who waved them through. The elevator door closed before he spoke again.

"Are you awake?"

"Of course. But it feels good to be carried." She looked around her.

The elevator door opened and, lo and behold, who was waiting for them outside but his dear wife. The real Mrs. Dallas. John scowled at her. Arms folded, she scowled back.

"Carrying your wife across the threshold, Dallas?" Kel greeted with heavy sarcasm.

The tone of her voice perked John's attention. My, but he finally got some positive reaction—he took note of the glare, the glint in those light hazel eyes, the set of her lips. Yes, yes, all the signs of a jealous woman.

He stepped out of the elevator. "Do show me the bridal suite, dear executive secretary." He smiled.

Kel continued glaring at him, then turned around, marching down the carpeted hallway.

John followed, his smile widening as he studied the stiff back of the woman ahead. She was wearing a pair of old jeans that clung to her in all the right places, and he eyed them appreciatively. He used to love seeing Kel in jeans. Guessed he still did.

The suite was huge. He immediately noticed that it had several bedrooms. He settled the very quiet Zaleiha onto the expensive-looking brocade sofa. Her eyes were still round as saucers as she looked about her.

Kel leaned against the well-stocked bar nearby, her eyes glittering. "Nice, dutiful husband," she mocked. "The call from the lobby a moment ago said that Mrs. Dallas was suffering from the heat. I don't see any such thing."

"She was hysterical."

"Sure she was. Heat can make a woman like that. She sure looks hysterical now too," Kel came back, disbelief in her voice.

"It was the ride from New Delhi that frightened her," John explained amiably. He was enjoying this jealous Kel a lot.

"We came this close to hitting some cows!" informed Zaleiha, thumb and finger emphasizing the danger they'd been in. "I was so frightened, and John comforted me. He is a very nice man to hug."

"Uh-huh," said Kel.

"I'd better go down to reception to finish signing us in," John said. This was the perfect moment to let the woman stew. Now Kel knew how he'd felt for the last few days. "Care to fill me in about what I need to do?"

Kel's sideways glance was expressively clear about what she thought he needed to do. He grinned. Things were looking up; he was the one screwing with her mind this time. "I can do that later," he continued, and studied her luscious figure, "but business before pleasure, and all that."

"Did you check up on your next assignment?"

"I did a lot of checking up," John told her, and this time he watched her closely. "I've quite a few questions for you, Kel Dallas."

She blinked at the sound of her married name. It sounded strange to him too, but certainly not as strange as he'd thought. And, most importantly, she hadn't mentioned anything about changing it back to Kel Grant.

"Questions later. You're a VIP guest here," Kel said, as she walked into the room. She handed him an envelope. "All the IDs you need right now. What did you tell them about not being here for the Taj Mahal trip?"

John shrugged as he tore open the envelope. "Delays, whatever."

"Go down and leave a message for Dr. Dante. Follow the instructions in the envelope."

"Yes, ma'am. I want to do things exactly your way."

She snorted. "I doubt that's what you want, Dallas."

He wanted to kiss her, actually. But that wasn't in the instructions. He had a feeling if he kissed her right now, he would forget to go downstairs. Besides, there was Zaleiha. "We're finally here, Za. Where's your big hug for your friend Kel?"

Zaleiha was looking at them like they were both wild beasts. "You had better make some coffee for her," she advised. "She has the same evil look in her eyes that you did the morning I first met you."

"Like a drunk donkey?" John asked helpfully. When Zaleiha nodded, he added wickedly, "Sorry, Za, coffee won't do it. There's only one way to soothe Kel."

Zaleiha's face went red. "Oh," she squeaked.

Kel was scowling again. Oh, he was enjoying this. Let's see her stew in her own juices.

"See ya both in a bit," he called out, as he strode out of the suite.

The moment he was in the elevator, he pulled out the envelope. The information was the usual deal. His next job. Yet, there was an odd feeling about the whole thing. His instincts told him the last few assignments were connected somehow. If only he could see past the obvious. But he must be doing something right, or they wouldn't have sprung Kel on him.

Twice. Twice, after three years. He chewed on his lower lip, as the lift descended back to the lobby.

Did she know how much she affected him? Was that why they sent her—so he might be distracted for a while?

He frowned at that thought. Mostly because he *had* been distracted.

There were several bedrooms up there and he'd lock both of them in one. The elevator door opened with a quiet hum and he exited, giving the security guard an absent-minded smile, his mind on the woman upstairs. He had plans for his own personal version of an information exchange.

It took him quite a while to get to the registration desk. Security was tight, what with so many important people within the walls of the hotel. He wondered whether the people working at the desk were really employees; their smiles of welcome were a bit too fixed.

He copied the message he'd read in the elevator onto a piece of hotel paper, folded it, and asked the desk clerk to make sure to put it in Dr. Dante's box. He gave the man twenty rupees for his trouble. If the clerk was really an undercover agent and snuck a peek, it'd read just like an innocent business message. This Miklos Riman Dante guy sounded familiar.

He strolled down to the lower area of the lobby, taking his time looking through the gift shops and boutiques. It was good to be alone again. He wasn't good with female company, never had been. The days with Zaleiha had taken a lot of patience. She had so much to learn about life outside a mountain village, and although she was a quick learner, he wasn't cut out to be her tutor. What the hell was the Temple going to do with her? Undoubtedly, she had to fit somewhere in their maze of plans, or they wouldn't have gone through the trouble of giving her a new identity.

Seven years he'd been at this, and he had never even been close to actually stripping the veil of secrecy from the Temple. Everything was perfectly camouflaged, surrounded by layers of different dummy corporations. Hell, it was they who'd shown him how to start Knights Inc., an international import-export business specializing in antiques, even though he was nothing more than a glorified rogue treasure-hunter. He'd plunged into the strange world of finance, stolen artifacts, and government intrigue. The following years had made him very cynical about the power structures that held the world together—most of them, it seemed, controlled by a handful of men.

On the outside, he was CEO of Knights, Inc., a businessman who dealt in war artifacts, someone who financed a number of archaeological digs around the world, a low-key figure who made his money selling treasures to a selected few who belonged to the elite of the world. On the inside, he was a double agent, for The Temple and for Uncle Sam. There was no easy way to describe what the Temple really was. Uncle Sam sure didn't understand, but what Uncle Sam knew was that it was useful to have someone on the inside. The Temple negotiated for different groups of people who wanted to be anonymous, sometimes for treasure, sometimes for people, sometimes for politics. And the United States government was interested to know the details, or as much information as John Dallas, ex-military, ex-CIA man, supplied them with. They'd contacted him asking for the favor ever since they'd found out where he was working, using his long time friends to curry favors.

Ex-CIA. No such thing.

He'd discovered that one was never truly retired from covert work. Call it the seven-year itch but he'd been getting restless lately. The Temple, in the beginning, was a challenge, a personal Mount Everest. Like the mountain, operatives had been sent up and defeated. However, nobody had been in there as long as he had—the former military man with an interest in treasure-hunting. He'd introduced himself to them as a modern day Indiana Jones. Now, because of his success these past years, he was virtually autonomous in his dealings with them.

In fact, John had more questions than Uncle Sam. Seven years, and all they'd ever contacted him about were weapons and people exchanges. Sure, the treasure quests were fun, but that wasn't enough for him any more, but they'd only led to more questions. Why the interest in treasures? And why were some pieces so important? So, instead of keeping a low profile and simply following orders, he'd started to push a little more.

Mount Everest wasn't totally insurmountable. A few people *had* reached its peak. He just needed to make it his quest. At this point of the game, he didn't really care what Uncle Sam wanted. He was in charge of a group of highly-trained soldiers-of-fortune. He'd even made his own fortune.

What were they going to do, fire him?

***

Kel heard the door to the suite open exactly one hour twenty-five minutes after John had left. She hadn't been worried when he departed. John would be able to get out of any sensitive situation. Plus, she could tell from the evil gleam in his eye he liked having the upper hand again. Trying to keep herself occupied, she worked on some files at the laptop.

She looked up from her work at the desk, pretending to be surprised. The evil gleam that shone in those black eyes always managed to give her a girlish shiver. He had a way of looking at her as if he were assessing every intimate secret in her mind. The dare-devil glint challenged her every female instinct to yield to him.

She jutted her chin out as he approached. She wanted so much more from this man, but she wasn't sure whether he was capable of giving it to her.

"Worried about me?" he asked, coming to a stop in front of her.

He was much too close. Whirling the chair from the desk, she tilted her head back and met those eyes again. Dark, devilish...and yes, desire was in there too. She remembered that look only too well.

"Should I be?" she countered. "You're probably just trying to get back at me for what happened in Pakistan."

"Damn straight." He moved even nearer, still not touching her. "What was that all about Kel? Really kinky, but not really a reunion, surely."

"Wedding," Kel reminded him.

"Wedding, reunion, whatever you want to call it," John said, his voice soft. "You know you didn't have to knock me out."

"Would you have let me go off the next morning?"

"You'll never know now, will you?"

He leaned forward, putting his hands on either arm of her chair, trapping her. His body heat surrounded her and she breathed in his masculine scent. Why was it that the mere mixture of body temperature and chemical essence could heighten all her senses? When he was near her like this, her sight, her sense of smell, her hearing—every part of her—was focused entirely on his being.

"It wasn't something I wanted to fight over," she explained, her voice husky. "I had a limited amount of time to spend with you and you were going to ask too many questions."

"So you had your way with me and just left? Did you know we were going to meet again here, or were you going to wait another three years before contacting me?"

The slight edge in his voice was the only thing that hinted at his mood. Everything else about him was very controlled, as if he had made up his mind not to lose his temper. Kel wouldn't have expected any less from him; his skill at negotiations was legendary.

And he was in full battle mode now, trying to find the chinks in her armor, looking for a way to invade. He was definitely not going to play hide and seek with her anymore. She had been prepared for this, yet she still felt the tiny flutters of nervousness in the pit of stomach. A big dose of John Dallas after years of starvation wasn't easy on a woman's peace of mind.

"There was a chance that I would see you again," Kel told him, deliberately needling him.

She noted the slight narrowing of his dark eyes. "Anyhow, I knew you'd come after me sooner or later, whether it was after your next assignment, or the next, but you wouldn't have left things as they were. As luck would have it, you were at the border, and easily available for this job in India."

"As were you," John remarked in a dry voice, pointing out the convenience of it all. "And that tribal dude, Ahmin seems to know that as well."

She smiled at his sarcasm. He was mad because she was right. He would have gone after her, one way or another. "I knew you'd sacrifice something to come here; that was a given." She had to tease him a little. "Of course, Ahmin would have made it."

"Who is he? I'm willing to bet he isn't with that tribe all the time"

She shook her head. "He's part of a US covert group gathering up stolen weaponry. A useful source and a good ally."

Ahmin had had come to her aid several times already. It was easy to help him this time, getting Kaleiha out of that village.

"Is he my back up, then?"

She loved teasing him, getting his back up. "Well, there *was* a slight chance you wouldn't make it. A big earthquake might somewhat delay you, for instance. Acts of God do sometimes interrupt our operations, you know."

"Or if I had quit."

Quit the Game? John? She raised an enquiring brow at the notion. "Sorry, that doesn't compute since our last big quarrel had to do with your loving the game too much. I believe your words were 'Can't leave it, darling. Don't make me choose between you and the Game right now.' Remember?"

That had hurt. And because it hurt so much, she had pushed him, giving him an ultimatum.

It might have been years but the pain of leaving him had stayed with her. What happened next *had* been an act of God. She had left him, thinking he would follow, and then—as the saying went—shit happened. The choices after that weren't hers anymore.

He studied her silently and she looked back at him, letting him draw his own conclusions.

It wasn't easy staying one step ahead of him, and she knew that everything she told him would be filed away for later use. John Dallas was a consummate analyst, a necessary trait in the art of negotiation.

She had to be very careful with every revelation. What she needed to do, first of all, was to negotiate a truce of some sort. She had to be prepared for the barrage of questions coming her way. And, she admitted, with both trepidation and thrill, to be the target of some very intense attention.

The thrill was easily explained. After all this time, John still made her weak all over. She was so attracted to him, she ached from wanting him. No, she didn't need to hide how she felt about him; she couldn't even if she wanted to. All he had to do was lean forward now and kiss her, and she would willingly wrap her legs around him. As she thought about this, he moved even closer, until her only choice was to look into his eyes. Her heartbeat thundered

"Kiss me," she whispered softly.

"Not yet," he told her, just as softly.

"Why?"

His breath was hot against her lips. "Because you keep asking me to remember this and remember that. I want you to remember something else."

"What's that?" His proximity was driving her insane. She wanted to jerk him closer somehow, but felt paralyzed by the sensuality of his gaze.

"I want you to remember that you asked me to give you more than you were willing to give me. I want you to feel this between us and realize you gave it up for ambition. You walked away from us because you couldn't wait. You put distance between us because you were afraid.

He couldn't have been more wrong. Kel didn't blink once through his accusations. Yet there was truth in his wrong conclusions. She forced a small smile.

"How like a man to pick and choose what to remember and what to forget," she mocked. "Was what I asked so much? And just because I took another position within the organization must mean I did so out of blind ambition and fear, of course. If it were a man you'd have said 'Way to go! Go for it!' You're a male chauvinist pig, John Dallas! If I were a man..."

"If you were a man, we wouldn't have been lovers and you wouldn't have given me an ultimatum!" John retorted.

"If I were a man, we wouldn't be married," she finished.

"If you were a man, we wouldn't have been allowed to marry in front of an imam," he told her, a small smile tugging his lips. "Now that we've established you aren't a man, why don't you tell me exactly why you married me and what is this game we're playing? Because, you know, it'd help me to understand the situation a whole lot better. Let's start with us."

"This is my final assignment," Kel said, watching his face closely.

"Your final assignment was...to marry me," John said rhetorically, his tone of voice deceptively casual.

Kel grinned. "No, my final assignment was to find the treasure that Dante wants. But marrying you was the opportunity to pull you close to me."

He studied her for a minute. "Not once in the last three years, Kel..." he began.

Kel held up a silencing hand. She took a deep breath. Coming clean was more difficult than she'd imagined. The look in his eyes. The way his head cocked to one side when he was considering something serious. The scent of him being so near. Everything she'd ever wanted was standing in front of her. She couldn't chance losing him. Rules be damned. This once, maybe love should rule her head, not the moves of the game.

"Remember how you were to train me in all aspects of hostage negotiation and exchange?" she asked softly.

The change of subject made him frown. "Yes."

"What did you think at that time?"

He thought about it a moment. "That it was strange they chose me. Usually that falls into the hands of a few other Knights. And I was suspicious for a while because they told me you were to be a courier. I finally figured they didn't actually mean a lowly pawn courier when you showed all the signs of having high clearance."

Kel nodded. "I'm going to show you something," she said, "and I don't want you to freak out. I just want you to hold on to your temper long enough to hear me out."

He cocked his head. "This sounds bad."

It could be, for her. In spite of herself, her training repeated the mantra of the game in her head. Risk. Options. Move. A strategic and safe advance. She mentally crossed her fingers as her hands reached up to the front of her shirt. His gaze caught hers then, turned watchful as she started to undo the buttons. His eyes widened and his breath caught when she lifted one side of the material.

"What the hell...."

He came closer and reached out. His hand touched her gently, his finger tracing the outline of her tattoo. He went down on his haunches to study it. He tilted his head and his eyes were very fierce.

"Tatt...it's a bird of some kind but its head...what the hell happened to you? Who shot you?"

Kel smiled at the dark emotion in his gaze. "It's shrapnel from an explosive. Someone tried to kill me but fortunately, I managed to get out before.... No, don't say anything yet. You're getting all demanding again and not paying attention. Look at the phoenix's tail."

His mouth clamped shut into a grim line as he looked down again. She resisted running her fingers through his thick hair. His finger continued tracing her tattoo—not new any more, but new to him. She'd chosen this design because of what the phoenix represented. Rebirth. For her, a second chance.

It was a beautiful tattoo. When it was healed, she'd looked at it constantly, touching the scar tissue and oddly finding comfort in it whenever she remembered her close call. She had gotten used to it now, barely noticing its presence when she wasn't in front of a mirror.

The phoenix head was deformed because even tattoo needles couldn't hide the ugly scar, two inches across, almost quarter of an inch deep, marring her once smooth skin. The artist had wanted to design the tail over that area, but she'd insisted the head be placed there—a reminder, she'd told him, of the danger of fire and death, even in a rebirth—and after a dubious look, he'd complied with her wish.

The tail flared out a gorgeous design of bold red, blue, green and purple. Hidden among the peacock-like feathers was a tiny crown of Celtic knots. It flowed with the intricate peacock design and only a practiced eye would see it. She heard another intake of breath from John and knew he'd discovered it.

Again, his gaze lifted. Incredulity. Questions. He stood up and started pacing the room. She could tell he was busy trying to put two and two together.

"The Queen is dying," Kel continued. "Not immediately, but it's a medical condition. I'm one of her possible...successors."

"When did you know this?" he asked quietly.

"Not at first, when they were sending me all over the place to train, but I was suspicious I was being prepared. Then, while I was with you, I found out the truth when they confronted me about our involvement." She sighed. Rebuttoning her shirt, she turned back to her desk. "Things happened all at once. We quarreled. Someone who was in the running tried to get rid of me with a bomb. And then, months of recuperation. In the end, they gave me an ultimatum. Exposing you of your double agency and getting you in trouble with your men or continuing my path."

John made a sound and she found herself swirled around by strong hands. His watchful expression had turned angry. "Why didn't you just tell me? I waited for you to come back, Kel. A word, and I'd have been at your side."

She laid her hands on his chest. "I was injured," she reminded him gently. "Shrapnel and a collapsed lung. I wasn't in any shape to do anything. Except for one thing."

He shook her slightly. "You chose to protect me."

She nodded. "They had the advantage in that particular game. I couldn't warn you or stop them from exposing you, so I chose to continue as understudy to successor. It was part of the deal. No communications. John, until confirmation that I made it as successor or not. And if I wasn't chosen in the end, I wasn't allowed to tell you what I've been doing either.

"I was on the list to be in the top tier and it isn't easy to quit them. Sure, I was ambitious, but you meant more to me, and even when I was weak as baby, I saw a way out. I would play a long game with them, with you as my winning piece." She smiled at him. "I figured power would protect you. If I play their game and win, my wish is their command, and my wish is to keep you safe."

"I know now why you drugged me. You didn't want me to see that tattoo."

She nodded. "It wasn't the right time to answer your questions. I needed to get Leiha and the message out, prove to them I could do my job with you around me. It wouldn't have been possible if you'd known the truth. It was a test for me."

He was silent for a long moment, his eyes searching hers. "True," he finally admitted, "The orders to get married threw me. And then I saw you and knew you had something to do with it. I only went through it because it was you."

"We aren't really legally married. It was just my way to tell you how committed I am to be with you. I can still say those magic words to free you."

"Three years, Kel. Three fucking long years.

"I know."

"I can't forgive that. Not yet."

"I know."

There was another short silence. "This last game. How does it figure into their plans for you?"

"If we win, I'm free," she told him. "We can be together and there won't be repercussions. I've protected you all along, can't you see? You think they don't know

61

you're passing on information to the government? Don't be naïve, John."

"What if we don't win?"

She knew she had to tell the truth. And she didn't want to hurt him. "There's a chance they won't honor our agreement if I fail to deliver," she said, then shrugged. "I've never thought beyond the promise of us. It's up to you now. Do you want to take the chance?"

She glanced up quickly and found his dark eyes still focused intently on her.

"I've always wanted you, Kel, and I don't intend to let you go. I want to get to know you again. Things have changed; we've changed. That I still want you might not be enough. You're going to be the Queen. Excuse me while I take some time to process the shock."

"The most important thing for me is whether you want to stay with me this time."

"If you were a man...no. Fuck their manipulative game."

"Then let's leave this decision till we've finished the assignment," Kel suggested. He wanted her. She could make him love her again. "No promises until you're sure. That's all I'm asking, John."

She let the hope shine from her eyes. She wanted him to see how much this meant to her

Time with him. Time to explain. Time to heal. Second chances were so rare and she was going to grasp at hers like a drowning woman after a lifeline.

"You're so lucky you're not a man, Mrs. Dallas."

Her heart thundered at his soft words. The look in his eyes made her weak in the knees. Come what may, she'd always treasure this moment.

"So, since I'm not a man, why are you still talking and not kissing me?"

His eyes narrowed. "Good question," he murmured, and dipped his head.

THE END

SEX LIES & SPIES

SHORT VIGNETTES IN THE LIVES OF SPIES.

EACH NOVELLA OF THIS SERIES IS A SHORT STORY
SHOWING
SECRET MOMENTS BRINGING TWO SPIES TOGETHER

THIS EPISODE FEATURES A MALE/MALE ROMANCE

THE PAWN

*This episode features a male/male couple. Hot intimate scenes ahead.

Cramped *The quality of a Chess position that inhibits freedom of movement for pieces behind Pawns of the same color. A cramped position lacks space. When a player's position is cramped, then that player has less freedom of maneuver than his opponent. A player that is cramped cannot switch the play from one side of the board to the other as quickly as his opponent*

CHAPTER ONE

Fuck. Of all the gay bars in the whole fucking world, Big, Tall and Dangerous had to come into his. He wasn't hard to notice, standing a head taller than most men, muscular, handsome and striking admiration, fear and in his case—lust—in the hearts of men everywhere. There was a small murmur among the guys when he first entered that made Svenni look up from his drink.

The drink hung midair between bar and lips when he saw who they were admiring. Fucking sex-on-a-stick, his favorite straight-guy-he'd-like-to-bang fantasy, Martin

Branson. Six-foot-five on a frame he knew from once watching him at a poolside to be all meat and no fat, broad on top, narrowing down to lean hips. Powerful thighs that gave him more fuel for his fantasies. Svenni remembered trying not to stare at the revealing bulge between them.

Now that particular fantasy strode in and the small group of men by the entrance parted like the Red Sea. What the fuck was he doing here?

Branson's head turned right and left, ignoring a couple of interested young things patting his big arms. He was seeking and it wasn't for casual male loving. Therefore, he must be looking for him.

Svenni tossed down his tequila, jumped off his stool and headed for the back entrance. He tried to duck down but damn it all to hell, it was difficult to be unnoticed when he himself was taller than most and, this early, there was no crowd into which to disappear. Worse, there weren't many men with bright blond hair like his. Not in this bar in Estonia, anyway. Damn it all to hell and back.

He gave a quick glance over his shoulder, caught the hulking man's direct stare, turned, and started running. No time. He'd left his piece in his car and anyway, shooting was bad form in this place. Even if he made it out unscathed, the owners would kill him the next time he was in town.

Pushing the few surprised guys out of the way, Svenni powered towards the exit behind the curtains near the stairway. He jumped at the roar coming right behind him, the sounds of scattering bodies and overturned stools, and just as he reached the sparkly waterfall curtains, a big male hand curled around his neck and pushed him through.

In the badly lit passageway, he lunged backwards, using his head as the weapon, but it was no use. His reflex and timing were slowed down by alcohol. The male hand around his neck moved and he found himself in a choke hold as a big body crashed him into the wall. Fighting for balance, he elbowed backwards, but his assailant anticipated that too, and before he could find his feet, Svenni found himself pinned, his arms painfully locked behind his back, his hands twisted in an unbreakable and painful hold.

He felt something slipped around his wrists, tugging hard. Caught. And tied.

Fuck.

"Well, well, well. A little early to be in here, Svenni, isn't it?" The man spoke softly, his warm breath teasing his ear.

Svenni tried to turn his head but it was difficult when his cheek was mashed up against the wall. His tequila-addled brain noticed stupid things. Like the well cut masculine lips so close to his own. And the clean cologne mingled with musky male scent. He shook his head, cursing at himself for having been caught. He'd thought he'd covered his tracks well.

"It's never too early too fuck," he said, injecting as much nonchalance as he could into his voice. "What are you doing here, anyway, Branson? Nothing in this place for you."

"Oh, I wouldn't say that."

A hand reached down between his legs and squeezed. Svenni choked. What the—. Fingers pulled down the zipper of his cotton pants. A hand slipped inside.

"Hmm. I'd say there's a thing or two I want in this place."

Confusion and astonishment made him speechless. This was the last thing he'd expected from—before his scrambled brain could even comprehend what was happening, he was swung around. A shoulder stuck into his midriff and he was lifted up in the air. His astonishment grew. He vaguely wondered how Branson managed to do that while holding on to his dick, but hell if he wasn't being carried off like some war prize.

Svenni opened his mouth, then closed it again when he realized they were going back through the curtain, into the bar area. He twisted his body hard. The hand around his dick tightened in warning. He froze.

"Damn American. What's the problem?" A voice to his left, out of his line of sight, asked. It sounded like Dimitri, one of the owners.

"Need to borrow your keys to your place, D. Lover's tiff, that's all."

Svenni choked again. Lover's tiff? He heard the clang of keys being tossed.

"Here. You better not ruin my place."

The stairs creaked underneath their combined weight. From his upside-down position, Svenni looked down at the faces staring up after them. He could see several of the twinks fanning themselves. A few made lewd gestures. No one, it seemed, cared that he was a prisoner. And yet he couldn't bring himself to yell for help.

It was shock, that was all. Branson here, in this place, carrying him up the stairs to what he knew were private rooms, wasn't making sense at all. Did he think he could beat him up and get him to talk up there? And his hand—

"Fucking American. No finesse at all," Dimitri called out in Estonian.

Voices followed their ascent.

"Oh, I don't know. I wish I were Blond Boy."

"The Yankee has big hands."

"I bet he's just as big somewhere else."

"I wondered if Blond Boy would share?"

Svenni heard the giggles and lewd remarks as the semi-darkness swallowed them. His mind was racing. Of all the scenarios he'd envisioned, this was not one of them. Well, not a real-life scenario, anyway. This was part of a fantasy, the kind he allowed when he was half-asleep in bed, with his hand a loving companion. His cock. In Martin Branson's hand. He must have fallen asleep somewhere and was dreaming this.

Upstairs smelled of booze and sex. And other mind-bending things.

A door clicked open and a burst of cool air hit him as his captor walked through the door, still silent. The door shut by itself, a soft thud that sent an unexpected shiver down Svenni's spine.

The room was dimly lit, casting a soft red glow. A quick whirl and he found himself dropped onto a flat surface. A surprised *ooooph* came out of his lips and he blinked.

Branson stood over him. The bastard wasn't even out of breath. And damn it to hell one more time if his own dick wasn't standing up even harder at the bigger man's scrutiny. A small smile tugged at his lips as he kept looking.

"Enjoying the view?" Svenni asked rudely.

"Yes."

The reply shocked him into silence again. He cleared his throat. "But...you aren't gay. You have a girlfriend."

"Had. She and I broke up a month ago," Branson told him absently, as he leaned down.

Svenni kicked. His leg was easily swatted away, then caught. He swung his other leg up, trying for a scissor hold. Branson was stronger and faster than he'd thought, dodging his attack and then pulling his limbs and sliding his lower body about as if he didn't weigh anything. In seconds, he found himself unable to move an inch, no matter how hard he tried.

A brown hand reached down and started unbuckling his belt. He went still, his mind still unable to process what this meant. He broke out in a sweat as he watched strong hands pulling off his pants. This must be a joke. It *had* to be a joke. He'd known Branson for three years, bumping into him numerous enough times, and had never seen him act anything but straight. Women gathered around him like bees to honey and he'd seen the guy checking them out with the usual male interest.

But right now, there was no time to figure it out. *Other* things demanded his immediate attention.

"I like a man with silk underwear. Easy to tear...like this," Branson murmured, stepping forward, forcing his legs open. One hand ripped at the flimsy elastic. "There. Let me show you one of the things I want."

Struggling was a lost cause. The fucker was standing on his pants, his stance just wide enough that Svenni couldn't kick them off. His heart boomed so loudly he was sure it was going to pop out of his chest. Never had he felt this helpless in front of a man. Nor this excited. Usually, he was the bigger one and it was tough to play out his own sexual fantasy when his partner could not hold him down like this one was doing without any problem.

He squirmed as fingers touched his perineum. Branson climbed up on the bed, his knees against the back of his thighs, effortlessly pushing his body back as his legs, tangled up with pants, lifted, providing heady access to probing fingers.

Svenni arched up, unable to curb his response. All the years of pent-up want surfaced and pulled at him like a riptide. A throaty groan escaped his lips when the exploration started on his eager crack of his ass.

He watched, fascinated, as a tube of KY appeared out of nowhere in one of Branson's hands. The man must be a magician—where the hell did that come from—and then all thought became unimportant at the unmistakable sound of another pair of pants being unzipped.

"Fuck!"

Branson paused. "Yes, I'm about to do that." His voice held the mocking amusement that always made Svenni want to cuff him.

"Why are you doing this?" He squirmed, trying to free his tied hands. No go. "What the fuck are you up to? I mean, you didn't come here for this. You've been sent to take me to somebody, haven't you?"

"Yes, but you're looking too delectable, all tied up and helpless. Besides, I'm free to do what I want now. Taking you this way first then taking you in. Win-win for me." Branson leaned even closer, forcing Svenni's thighs further apart, his face inches from his. "Tell me you don't want me and I'll stop."

Unable to stop himself, Svenni arched up, even as he panted out, "I don't. Want. You." He flushed at the taunting laughter. He could feel something hot against his anus, something he needed inside him. "You aren't my type."

"No? How come your cock is making a hole in my stomach?"

Pressure. Martin Branson was pushing his cock up his lube-slicked channel. The pain and pleasure of being taken with such sureness excited him unbearably. Terrified him. Not knowing why it was happening escalated the feelings a hundred-fold.

"Tell me no and I'll pull out."

Svenni stared up into the dark eyes looking back at him so damn solemnly. He barked out a short laugh. "You got your cock in me and *now* you're trying to be considerate?" His voice sounded feverish. He needed more of it inside. Touch him in the right place, baby. "Fuck you, Branson. Fuck. You."

"You have the worst mouth, you know that? I think I'll shut you up now."

A hand held his jaw firmly. Branson angled his head and his lips locked unerringly onto Svenni's. A tongue slipped into his mouth. In his fantasies, he'd often wondered what Branson tasted like. Coffee and brandy and something indefinable, something that was addictively delicious. The lazy exploration of that wicked tongue was arousing beyond belief, enhanced by his inability to escape.

Another throaty moan escaped him as the cock inside him started thrusting deeper. Holy fucking Batman. The man's cock must be as big as his feet. So...good. The thrusts were slow and easy, taking the time to adjust him to his size.

Svenni couldn't believe how being so absolutely helpless was turning him on like this. Two hundred forty or more pounds of pure muscle held him prisoner, chest to chest. Even his mouth was a captive, letting the other man's tongue do whatever it wanted.

The big body above his changed position slightly and the angle of his thrust shifted. *Oh yes. Oh God yes.* He'd been wanting that, waiting for that. The big rod slid over his prostate gland and nudged that magic spot. He could feel the slow sizzle gathering up the back of his spine, the pulse-starting to pound at the base of his own cock, knotting tighter as Branson thrust in and out.

Steely fingers caressed the length of his cock and a calloused thumb rubbed his precome all over the head, driving him crazy as it moved back and forth over the slit. Svenni groaned again. He felt on fire, his blood pooling molten hot in his engorged erection, his ass building a slow burn from the invasion. Branson released his lips and buried his face in Svenni's neck, nibbling his Adam's apple. He shuddered as each erogenous point tightened with helpless need. The thrusts became harder, pushing his body even further up the bed. It wasn't a comfortable position at all and Svenni could care less. His impending orgasm took precedence over all.

He mewed like a baby as that sizzling rubbing inside him became a roaring fire. He was burning up. He couldn't stop making those sounds as he tried to keep up with each wave rolling through him. The big cock sliding in and out of him was merciless, angling and caressing him inside over and over until the white heat at the base of his balls tightened and took him over.

He gasped as his body shook with pleasure, each orgasmic wave cresting and crashing until he couldn't catch his breath any more. He was aware Branson was breathing hard too before one last stroke took him over. His lover came quietly, his head thrown back, revealing a strong, brown throat.

Svenni closed his eyes, breathing in the musky scent of sweat and sex. The fan above hummed. The sheets under his body felt cool against his hot skin. His heart rate was slowly returning to normal and he could feel his own breathing following Branson's even one. His brain cells must be working again because questions started to flood his mind like rapid fire.

What the hell just happened?

Why was Branson sent to come after him? Oh, he knew what he was after, but why Branson?

How the hell was he going to get out of this pickle?

And most important of all, how did he miss the fact that Martin Branson, god of all tall, dark, and imperious, liked guys?

That last question flashed like a neon sign—over and over—and he still couldn't get over the shock of this new knowledge.

The man in question moved and Svenni felt him sliding out of him. The warmth on his body lifted. He clamped down on the niggle of disappointment. He wanted more. He opened his eyes and silently watched as Branson got off him and slid out of bed.

"That was...nice," Branson said with a slight smile.

Nice? He'd show him nice. "Fuck you, you asshole."

"Really need to do something about that foul mouth of yours, Svenni." Branson looked around. "Be right back."

He sauntered off to another door to the left and disappeared through it. The sound of water. Must be the bathroom.

Svenni abruptly turned to his side and swung his legs over the side of the bed, working on his trapped hands. It wasn't metal handcuffs. Plastic tie. Sitting up, he quickly looked around him for a pair of scissors or something sharp. He stood up and immediately fell over, landing painfully on his knees.

Fucking-A. Sex had robbed him of all his ability to think straight; he'd forgotten about the pants still tangling around his legs. He struggled to get up but with no help from his hands, he toppled over like a tree. Grunting and cussing under his breath, he pushed up with his face as he tried getting back on his knees.

A short laugh came from behind. Svenni ground his teeth. Just kill him now.

A hand patted his butt and then reached under him. Something wet—a cloth?—came up against his privates.

"Your ass is up in the air. Another round already? I was going to clean you up but apparently you have other ideas."

A hand held on to his neck and his face scrunched against the carpet. "I'm beginning to dislike the way you keep smashing my face against things," Svenni muttered. "Enough of this. Help me up."

"Not on your life. This is too good an opportunity to miss."

"Branson..."

"My name's Martin, you know."

That would make all this happening too personal and Svenni didn't know enough to get personal with him right now. He was a prisoner, for crissakes. "Branson," he repeated, "Tell me what the fuck's happening. Why are you doing this?"

"I feel insulted. You don't know what's happening. Here, maybe I should just do it again and again until I get this right."

Svenni felt his butt cheeks being parted. "You aren't...damn it, Branson, get me off this fucking position."

"But you *are* in a fucking position. I might as well fuck you."

There was laughter in that voice even as Svenni felt slickness against his anus again. The still sensitive nerves tingled in delight as long fingers worked lube in and out. He shook his ass, hoping to dislodge the invasion, but again, his legs refused to budge because of those *damn pants*, and Branson's weight on them effectively kept him in position.

Svenni had never, ever, felt this vulnerable. He suddenly realized this man could do to him whatever he wanted. Fuck him senseless. He shivered at the thought. Would he?

It was unbearably exciting. Unbidden, his dark fantasies popped up, defeating him. The big Viking taking his war prize from behind. Being forced to be his sex slave. Having that big cock master him. And it all started again, the maddening want for a man who could take him and make him his. Just like that, his own dick was hard as a rock again.

Already, the finger was deep inside, preparing him, making him anticipate something bigger. Already, the buzzing at the base of his cock had started, as the finger knowingly tapped against that sensitive gland inside him. He whimpered.

"Yeah, like that," Branson whispered. "I know what you like, Svenni. Gonna take you again and this time I'm going to go deeper. You okay with that?"

Not that he was waiting for a reply. The finger was out and the replacement was unmistakable, scraping the still sensitive nerves. Branson's dick felt huge from this angle, almost too much. Svenni gasped as it slid deep inside, deeper than anything he'd ever experienced. He felt Branson's balls tickling his ass and gasped again as the man's weight forced him into the carpet, sheathing that delicious cock even deeper.

Two strong hands massaged his shoulders tenderly. "Ready?"

"You're killing me with laughter here."

"Smart-mouth." Amusement and arousal had deepened his voice into a dark, rich tone. "Admit it, you want this."

"Haha. Right. Whatever you say," Svenni said, although in a breathier voice than he planned, even as he pushed his ass up, meeting thrust for thrust. "Being tied up by you right now is just up my alley."

Another punishing thrust knocked the air out of him.

"Like I said, smart-mouth. But I wouldn't want you as much if you weren't such a cranky sonnovabitch."

The thrusts were timed just right. Quick in, slow out. Quick in, s...l...o...w out. The slide against his prostate was magical. His insides melted every time that languid pull went on forever. Then the hard thrust back would jolt his senses like electricity. He felt his own dick bobbing in and out of the mesh of the carpet, creating a secondary sensuous torture.

Smart-mouth and Cranky versus Tall, Dark and Fucking Big. Tall, Dark and Fucking Big was winning by a mile because Smart-mouth and Cranky was crying like a cat in heat, begging for release. He couldn't stop himself. At the edge and needing to come. But a hand was pulling at his balls, taking his attention away.

"My name." It was an order, softly spoken. "Say my name and I'll let you come long and sweet, lover boy."

No.

The slow and delicious slide out caused his guts to tremble, and then, the inevitable tightening around his balls.

No!

So near. He was being played like a violin with each stroke, making him beg for release. His resistance was pitiful. He whimpered as release eluded him again. The torture continued.

Oh, please.

No, don't give in!

Fuck, don't stop!

He made a half-hearted attempt to escape, trying to turn his body. Instead, the new angle just brought more contact with sensitive nerves. He made a guttural sound as his tormenter continued his assault, making approving noises at the change. The hand around his balls moved up and started jerking him off.

"My name, Svenni. Now." The demand was insistent, urgent.

Oh, please.

No, he won't dare sto—.

"Martin. Martin, Martinmart'nMar—ohshitMart'nMart—tin—Mar...tin...Mar...tin...Mart'n." Svenni chanted feverishly, ecstatically, as his come poured out of him, lava-hot.

* * *

Svenni told himself he was *allowing* the son-of-a-bitch to handle him, as he was helped back onto the bed. Shit, who was he trying to convince? After that mind-blowing session, he felt weak as a baby. Really, all he wanted to do was stretch out and savor the memory while drifting off to sleep. Maybe if he did that, he'd wake up and this would all have been some amazing wet dream, because then what just happened would make sense.

Because it still didn't make an iota.

He lay against the pillows quietly, enjoying the feel of the cool wet cloth dragging across his still-heated body parts. Martin Branson's hands moving all over, tucking in this, zipping up that. So damn proficient at it too.

He sighed.

"The silence is a nice change."

"I'm thinking," Svenni retorted, bringing his gaze back at Branson. "Processing information. Trying to figure you out."

The dark brown eyes mocked back at him. "Still need convincing, huh?"

He flushed. This new flirtatious Branson threw him off. "Are you going to explain or do you intend to make this a damn guessing game? Because, you know, my fate's kind of in your hands."

"That's a big word, fate. Do you think there's such a thing? Fate bringing you to me?"

Svenni studied his captor for a second. "You're insane, you know that? I'm talking about my current condition and you're turning it into some profound discussion. Oh, hell. You're not the kind who goes all deep and sentimental after a bout of sex, are you?"

The solemn look in the dark eyes disappeared and was replaced by amusement. "I thought you enjoyed my going deep."

"And stop flirting! It's...it's unsettling me."

"You flirted with me in the past," Branson pointed out.

Svenni shook his head. "That was before I knew you were—partly gay."

Branson laughed again, that rich deep rumble that warmed his insides. "So it was okay when you thought I couldn't possibly take you up on your many snide challenges?"

Svenni looked away. Point to Branson. He *had* been snide, often making off-colored comments, hoping to embarrass the man. He'd done it to cover up the pull of attraction. The guy's gorgeous girlfriend irritated him. Okay, he was jealous of her whenever she was around him. He recalled one particular incident. They were at an auction and at the before-party, groups had formed, and he'd of course found himself in the one Branson and his girlfriend were part of.

He'd told himself he was just doing his job, collecting names and information, and the girlfriend was a person of interest, so to speak, being an antiquities buyer. That Branson was hanging around was of interest too, since he knew of Branson being one of the "knights."

Knights, Inc., a group of mercenaries seeking out antiquities for collectors. Around these people, they were "treasure hunters," but the names Svenni had in his file belonged to men with enough special forces credentials to outfit a small army. Knights, Inc., was a cover and he was going to get some more information about them. If that meant sniffing around the equally gorgeous Mr. Martin Branson, well, that added a pleasurable torture he couldn't resist.

At that meeting, they'd been talking about one of the pieces being auctioned off. The buzz was there were more than the usual few interested parties and the guests were trying to figure out the anonymous buyers.

"Are you buying, Mr. Branson, or selling?" Svenni had asked.

"I'm just keeping Margaret company today," he'd replied. "What about you? Anything of interest lately that caught your attention, Svenni?"

It'd annoyed him that Branson was never formal with him, no matter how much he tried to put some kind of distance between them. Frustration had made him reckless. And daring. "One or two," he'd drawled, letting his gaze linger on the man's face before turning to smile at Margaret. "Just like you, I'm sure."

Branson had appeared not to notice the tension. His face held a polite expression of someone mildly interested in the conversation. "So you're going to try to outbid Margaret then," he said, without a single inflection in voice or face that might suggest he'd meant anything other than auctioned items.

Svenni had known he'd better back off because it was never a good idea to get people gossiping later about conversations they overheard at an auction. One never knew what would catch people's attention, but the adrenaline junkie in him was loose that day and he couldn't seem to stop himself.

"You never know," he'd said, still smiling because he'd thought himself so damn clever at that moment, having some fun teasing a straight guy because he could, "till you try."

That was months ago.

Had that challenge been taken up today, and his ass handed back to him, or what? Already, his body was aching for more. The sexual high with this man was dangerously addictive.

"It's all fun and games until someone decides to take you to bed, is that it? Do you go around talking sexy to men, then? Or is it just to straight guys because that's how you jerk off?"

Indignant, Svenni looked up. Was there a slight accusation in his voice? "Hey, who are you to tell me off? As far as I was concerned, you were the male companion to Miss Margaret Wyman, art collector. You never once gave any hint you were anything else but. Apparently," he said, his eyes narrowing thoughtfully, "you were playing a part like I was."

Branson cocked his head. "And what part were you playing? A corporate spy perhaps?"

"Why is that of interest to Knights, Inc.? It has nothing to do with *treasures*," Svenni threw back.

"Ah. Are you pretending you don't know about the knights now?"

"Is that what you guys call yourselves? But of course, so damn clever. Knights have always been associated with warfare, *weaponry* and treasures," Svenni mocked. He jerked when Branson petted his still sensitive bulge. "Hey!"

"Warfare, weaponry, and *hidden* treasures," corrected Branson, with a small smile. "But yes, you're right and that's why you're so interested in us. After all, you've done quite a bit of data-mining, collecting all that info in that file of yours. Tell me, what were you going to do with the flash drive, put it out there to the highest bidder? Can't be worth too much because, you know, it's pretty well-known I work with a bunch of ex-military and mercenaries."

"So why the need to send you to capture me? Your hunky bunch of men all afraid of my little flash drive. Let me guess, it's not the flash drive."

"Bingo. Does the name Miklos Riman Dante mean anything to you?"

Svenni could feel all the heat leaving his face. That was the last thing he'd expected.

"Jackpot again, I think," his captor said softly.

Knight Fork. *Using one piece to attack two of the opponent's pieces at the same time.*

CHAPTER TWO

Miklos Riman Dante wasn't a man with whom to trifle with. Svenni was stupid once, a long time ago, and stole from him. An Egyptian treasure map. Five hours with Dante was memorably painful. Fortunately for him, he'd managed to escape, or was allowed to—he couldn't decide—but he'd an aversion to anything Egyptian since.

"What about him?" Svenni now asked cautiously.

"He's hired Knights, Inc. to look for a map for him.

"What's that got to do with me?"

"He collects treasure maps. You stole one."

"I gave it back." Oh, Svenni hadn't wanted to but the older man's whip was very persuasive.

"And yet, you live. Which interests my boss, Svenni. How did you escape? Giving back a map wouldn't have been enough with Dante."

Svenni swallowed the bitter taste that had formed. "I'd rather not go down that memory lane, thank you," he said curtly. "And you don't have to tie me up for this interrogation. You could have just walked up and asked me. So, who the hell hired you to get me? And what do they want?"

"So many questions," Branson murmured. "You really think you'd be cooperative being interrogated?"

By you, yeah. But he'd rather die than admit that now. He was having a hard time trying to keep his head screwed on tight and focused on his current dilemma because his damn body was still demanding other things to be done to it. Things that had nothing to do with keeping his mind clear so he could get out of this mess.

"Well, I do have a negotiating ace. The flash drive."

"Ah. What if I told you it's Dante who wants you?"

Svenni tried to keep his face expressionless but he was pretty sure he turned white as the sheets on the bed. "I don't have anything he wants. Unless it's the info on the drive?" He cocked his head, studying Branson's face closely. "Now, that's an interesting thought, isn't it?"

"You're afraid of him."

It was a statement, not a question, and Svenni didn't deny it. He didn't see the need to. Miklos Dante had a certain reputation in the underworld.

"Yeah. If you've met him, you should know dude's not all there."

"Never met him. I might if my boss wants me to hand you to him."

Svenni arched his brows. "So I'm not being handed over immediately?"

Branson's smile was infuriatingly taunting. "No, my orders were, specifically, to keep you prisoner, make you answer a few questions, and to bring you in when I'm satisfied you're going to cooperate." He leaned temptingly closer. "I've done two of the three. Not satisfied yet, though."

Those words had the effect of live wire. His body was winning over his brain more and more. The man had a way of sounding sexy and threatening all at the same time, and Svenni imagined he was being enjoyed as a pawn in this particular cloak-and-dagger game on many levels.

All he'd suspected about Martin Branson—that he was not the man he presented in public—was turning out to be true. When he'd been reading all the information about him in the files, it hadn't jived out. Special forces. A short stint in the CIA before suddenly leaving. The sudden quitting from the Company just didn't ring true, what with the high security clearance, good recommendations and no scandals or black marks. Catching up on some of the operations of which he'd managed to procure more than declassified details suggested a man of action, with a quick mind and a certain kind of brashness needed to jump into deep waters.

Yet, the Branson Svenni met and knew these past few years was all suave and sophisticated. He'd even laughed at the thought of "that big and tall sex-on-a-stick" being called a treasure hunter among the arts circles. Mostly quiet, he appeared to be nothing but arm candy to his girlfriend. If he hadn't been told Branson was with Knights, Inc., he'd have dismissed the man as another kind of treasure hunter, the type looking for a rich heiress.

And yet—

Those damnably sexy but watchful eyes never failed to send his libido into overdrive. It felt like he was biding his time and it drove Svenni crazy trying to get a reaction from the man. And he always smelled so good when they were standing together, talking inanely about sports and the latest political news in between bid rallies for artifacts. Svenni had a sharp sense of smell and it was damn distracting having images of putting his nose in the neck of a six-foot five-ish muscular dude to inhale that delicious scent and risking being pummeled to death while holding a normal conversation.

He hadn't liked being made to feel that way. So he'd decided to find out more about Martin Branson, hoping to uncover enough dirt of scamming and cheating that maybe his own interest would flag. Nope. Fucking information just deepened the mystery around the man. And definitely elevated his attraction.

"I've always known there was this side of you," continued Branson. "All the chatter you bring in your wake was a cover."

"Like you're not showing a different side now," Svenni pointed out. "Never even suspected, especially after I read your file. Your history didn't include any male romances."

He knew he sounded snide again, but it wasn't everyday he was blindsided, and Branson's laughter was low and intimate.

"How about a deal? You answer a few questions and I'll answer a few from you about me."

"And freedom," Svenni added.

Branson shook his head. "Can't do that without my boss' say so. But I can recommend...better treatment."

Svenni grinned. "Is your boss handsome and a closet gay too?"

Branson shook his head again. "That smartass mouth again. Bet it gets you in trouble."

"Every time." Svenni shrugged. His smartass mouth, as Branson called it, had saved his ass a lot too. "So tell me something. What's in all this for you? What does Knights, Inc., want when they send you gallivanting around with an antiquities buyer as your girlfriend? And why—mmmph."

The rest of his words were cut off by Branson clamping a hand over his mouth. For a man of his size, he was quick as hell. Svenni didn't even see him move.

"So many questions. Let's establish some rules first," he said, then removed his hand. "One, I set the pace. Two, we don't have to answer if we don't want to. Three, every time I catch you in a lie I get to exact punishment."

"That's giving you quite a bit of advantage," Svenni said wryly.

"But of course. You're the prisoner, after all. And I hope you don't mind leaving the country. I have all the necessary papers to fly you out of Tallinn."

Svenni sat up, startled. "Wait a minute. What—where?"

"India."

"Why the hell India?"

"That's where my boss is celebrating his honeymoon. And before you go on about it, his wife is a woman who also happens to be his boss."

"Don't tell me. Your boss is a sub and his wife is his dom," Svenni retorted. "You knights are such a kinky bunch. Hurray, kinky Indian wedding involving naked knights in leather and chains."

His sarcasm was rewarded with a deep sigh and a long look. Svenni felt a surge of satisfaction. How about that? A reaction from the almighty captor. Maybe there was a chink in this knight's armor after all.

He was usually not this mouthy, but alcohol and good sex often put him in a good mood and right now, he could *not* afford to be in one and that made him extra cranky. Being tied up and flown out of the country? He needed to talk fast and think faster.

If it had been anyone else but Martin Branson who had shown up looking for him, he wouldn't have ended up in this situation. He was sure of it. He had been very careful. It was just the explosive surprises Branson brought along with him that had taken away all his usual wits, that was all. If he could turn around and surprise the big fella, maybe he'd get a chance to make a run for it.

Right now, the bastard was waiting for an answer. He seemed to be having fun tying his shoe laces together too.

"Okay, I agree to the terms," he said aloud, in a bored voice.

Branson looked up from his task of tying a bow. "Oh, you're done thinking?" he asked, striking the same bored tone.

He was going to use those shoelaces and strangle him. "Sure. Overrated and all that," Svenni said instead. "Quick unrelated question though. What if I need to go take a piss? You going to carry me to the bathroom and take out my dick for me? You seem quite good at that."

Branson's answering grin was infectious. "I was going to untie your shoe laces and drop your pants, but I'm not averse to your suggestion."

"Do you do that with all your male captives? Help them piss?"

"Only the ones with tight asses."

Svenni couldn't help grinning back. "You talk a lot more now that you're...umm...broken up with your girlfriend. Who would have thought you could be so witty?"

Branson walked to the fridge by the bed. Opening it, he scanned its contents. "Tequila your thing, isn't it?"

"If you're planning on loosening my tongue, you can forget about it."

He gave Svenni a brief glance. "I want a drink. If you can't take a couple more, just say so. I'll get you water...if there's any in here. Up to you."

Svenni showed him the tied hands. "A bit tough to throw back a drink with you, buddy."

Branson pulled out a bottle from the fridge, walked over to a nearby chair and sat down, arranging his legs comfortably on the small coffee table. He took a swig. Heavy-lidded, he studied Svenni as he took another.

Svenni held his gaze as he flopped back against the pillows. Staring at the view wasn't a hardship. He liked looking at Martin Branson, always had. Clothes liked the guy too. They hugged him at the right areas, not too tight and always casually creased. Like now, for instance. Even after a wild romp on the bedroom floor, the man looked as if he'd done nothing too strenuous. Svenni glanced down at his own rumpled pants and decidedly wrinkled shirt, with one button missing. Unlike himself, who *did* look as if he just had a wild romp.

"Three years ago," Branson started very softly, "I was given the assignment to be with Margaret Wyman."

That brought Svenni's attention back to Branson. Assignment? As in not a real romance?

"My immediate boss, John Dallas, told me he was given orders to find out who ordered a series of attacks on...our organization."

"So Knights, Inc. was being attacked?" Svenni asked.

"Not in the sense you're thinking. There are higher-ups, just like any organization. Imagine Knights, Inc. as part of a conglomerate. Our CEO, so to speak. I'm telling you this so you can better understand what's happening. To distill three years' work, Margaret Wyman buys treasures and sends them to mostly one customer. She also takes orders to send certain packages containing items to various locations."

"Stolen?" Not surprising for one of these Knights, Inc., people to embed one of their own. They had a good reputation of locating stolen treasures.

Branson shook his head. "No." He took another drink from the bottle. "You've always been so impatient."

"And you're a lousy story-teller. Get to the good part already." *Like, when did you notice me?* "By the way, damn fine acting. Three years. I've met with you—what—twenty times and never thought you anything but straight."

Branson tapped the bottle against the palm of his hand. "It bothers you, doesn't it, me having been with Margaret."

"Bothered? You mean, was I jealous?"

"Oh, I know you were jealous. I'm not blind. Couldn't miss the signs." Branson gave a small knowing smile. "Bothered, as in bothering you now, that you couldn't tell. That I didn't let you know I was interested."

Now he had Svenni's full attention. "Were you?"

"Oh yeah, I was interested." The smile widened. "You don't know how tough it was to ignore your flirting. There were a few times I'd thought of cornering you in one of the back rooms and having a quickie in the dark, but the risks of being found out by Margaret's spies kept me from even stealing a kiss or two "

Something in those dark, gleaming eyes unsettled him. Eyes that saw and knew too much about him and his needs.

Svenni swallowed. "Okay, I'll take that drink now."

Branson stood up and strode back to the bed. Svenni had never been helped to drink before, and it was disconcerting to have the bigger man cradling him and pushing the bottle to his lips. He tipped his head back and savored the liquid fire going down his throat.

"Enough?"

Svenni nodded, still unsure how to respond. Branson was acting like a lover, attentive and caring, but he'd also just revealed he could put on an act for three years, so this could all be some kind of bullshit game Knights, Inc., put him up to. He'd been around enough treasure-hunters and treasure aficionados to know there were quite a few weirdos out there.

Questions. He had to come up with good questions and get information to help him get out of this bind. But his tongue seemed to have lost control of all common sense.

"It wouldn't have been quick. Do you think I wouldn't have attacked you my own way?" If that had happened, he would have made sure it wasn't some fast grope in the dark. *But damn it, that was not the right question.*

"And it would have been what I wanted. But reckless and not the thing for me to do. Just why you were such a temptation. Now, you have to answer my question. What information did you get from the data miner here in Tallinn?"

Svenni shrugged. "Which one? There are so many." He shrugged again when he caught Branson's gaze. "Hey, you made the rules. I'm not giving up a friend's name just to satisfy your curiosity. What's in it for you and your gang of knights?"

Branson nodded. "Fine. His name is Konstantin and we know him well enough. He won't tell on you either, so I didn't bother going after him. Konstantin likes online role-playing games and is in the midst of a quest for treasure in this particular game. Do you know anything about that?"

Svenni frowned. Sure, Konstantin had a rep for that kind of thing but he was a hi-tech nerd and they all love online gaming.

"I don't really know him that well but we meet often enough that I'm aware of the online role-playing stuff," he said carefully. He hadn't seen any big deal about that quirk. "Right now, he's involved in an extensive medieval world that...has...knights." He cocked his head, still not sure, and added, "And you called yourself a...knight. This is sounding a bit crazy, you know that."

Branson nodded again. Took another swallow from his bottle. "Yeah. How about the info that the man behind the game is none other than Dante?"

Svenni closed his gaped mouth. He felt like a fish today, what with his mouth falling open so many times. "What the hell is he up to?"

"It's a highly involved game and we've been playing along. No, not me, I can't spend my days doing that shit."

"So...there are nerdy knights?" Svenni quipped.

Branson's lip curled up at one corner. "I'll tell them you said that." He shifted as his hand went into his pants pocket, digging for something. "Take a look at this and tell me what you see. Does it look familiar to you?"

A small dark object lay on his palm.

"Turn it over," Svenni said. "No, the other way. Yeah. The marks on it appeared on the treasure map I stole that one time."

"Are you sure?"

"Pretty sure. What are they?"

"Svenni, your theft happened years ago. How do you know these are the right symbols?"

"It's some kind of cuneiform. My...ahem...teacher taught me a system to memorize these things."

Branson raised an inquiring brow. "Teacher?"

"Teacher," Svenni replied firmly.

"He taught you to read cuneiform," he said skeptically.

"I wouldn't say that, but it's...umm...a method."

"A method."

It wasn't anything to be ashamed of, he told himself. "I had a thief master teacher. He...ah...specialized in documents but he couldn't read very well, much less ancient text. The only way he remembered important things was to make up his own language. He was very good at recreating maps and documents that way."

Branson held up the small object between his thumb and forefinger. "So what do you read this as?"

Svenni looked up at the ceiling tiles and sighed. He was so going to regret this. "Wine, men, sex, rock and roll."

There was a little pause.

"I suppose I could see how you think the first two look like W and M, the third one doesn't even look like S but how is that squiggle a rock and roll?"

Svenni stopped counting the tiles and returned his gaze on Branson's face. Although he looked a little amused, he was actually studying the symbols seriously.

"My teacher taught me the objective was to remember quickly, so one could form a memory of any kind of symbols. I was young, so he told me to always make up phrases I'd immediately remember and see. "

"Makes sense, but the third one just looks like an upside-down mushroom."

Svenni rolled his eyes. "Oh, wine, men, dick, rock and roll is such a catchy and memorable phrase."

"Fine. Sex. What about this last squiggle?"

"Look, you can't just stop in the middle of a phrase. Let's rethink this. If you use 'to be or not to be,' to remember these symbols, you can't just stop at 'to be or,' right?"

Branson frowned. "I wouldn't need to use that system and if I did, I wouldn't have used that phrase."

Obviously, the man had no imagination. "It's just a way to remember," Svenni said, exasperated. "Either you believe I remember what I saw or not, I don't care."

"Okay, fine. Wine, men, sex, rock and roll it is. If that's not the dumbest system for a thief—"

"Master thief to you, mister," Svenni interrupted. "And how would you phrase that in your head without anything to write with or a camera to take a pic of, huh?"

"I wouldn't have gotten caught."

"If that's not the dumbest attitude. You need a backup system. Try it, look at those symbols and see if my phrase doesn't stick."

"It's actually 'wine, women and song' or 'sex, drugs, rock-and-roll' so no, your phrase doesn't stick for me."

Of all the most thickheaded response. How did he do it? How did he always manage to make him want to beat him up and fuck him at the same time? "Can you untie me for a few minutes so I can bang your head against this headboard? You can tie me up again after that."

He was rewarded by a dazzling smile.

"I like making you spitting mad," Branson said. "It turns me on, watching you trying not to lose your cool at those parties and get-togethers when you didn't succeed at baiting me."

Svenni faked a yawn "No idea what you're talking about." This man was too dangerous for him, turning him on with mere words and smiles. Right now he was thinking of leaning forward and offering him a kiss. He wanted to taste that sexy mouth again and wondered what else it could do to other parts of his—hell, he was beginning to forget he was a prisoner. "So I answered one of your questions. Why do you need me in India? We could just do Skype with your boss and get this over with."

He needed to know who wanted his ass. He sincerely hoped it wasn't Dante. It'd been a while but even with his experience now, he didn't think he could easily escape a second time.

"You're afraid of Dante and think we're going to hand you over to him."

What the—was the guy a mind-reader too? "Are you?"

"He has sent out word to have you captured, you know."

Svenni frowned. "Why? It's been a long while to think of me all of a sudden." He jerked his chin toward Branson's hand. "It has to do with that thing, right? You avoided the question the first time. What's in this for Knights, Inc., and its bosses, or whatever they're called? Kings, Inc.?"

Branson gave a bark of laughter, turned and headed for the fridge. He laughed again, a velvety deep-throated chuckle that sent a shiver down Svenni's spine, as he took out another bottle.

"What's so funny?" Svenni demanded.

"Your clever imagination. I need another drink. But to set your mind at ease, my boss is actually planning on using you as bait to get Dante's attention. He's already after you, anyway, so we thought we'd get to you first."

"But why does he want me now?"

"Map, treasure, you—what connection?"

It was a simple question but the line of logic made it so clear. He, Svenni Jorgensen, was once a master thief's prodigy.

Branson's cell phone beeped three times. Stopped. His dark head turned sharply towards the window. And all of a sudden, hell exploded outside the windows, in the streets below.

***

The rat-tat-tat of gunfire reverberated against the thick walls. They were in the old part of Tallinn and the buildings were hundreds of years old. The explosions echoed through the streets and alleys like one of those long chains of Chinese fireworks they hang out of their balconies.

Svenni rolled off the side of the bed, ending up in another awkward position. He could hear the windows rattling. No bullets whizzed by. Nothing broken around him. From the space under the bed, he watched Branson's shoes approaching.

"Hey, take your fucking time," Svenni yelled. "It's just some kind of marching band down there, nothing important."

Brandon knelt down. His expression was stern but the corner of his lips betrayed that little amused twist again. "We have a little time. They daren't enter Dimitri's turf without starting a gang war."

"Oh, yeah, all the time in the world. Just let me hop downstairs with you, Sir Knight, holding a broom with my hands tied behind my back, to slay the dragon."

There was a flash of teeth and then Brandon was back up on his feet, hauling Svenni with him.

"I'll free you for now. You have two choices—fight with me or fight on your own. I've to point out that they're after you, not me, even though they thought they could search my car while I'm occupied in here."

"That beeping from your phone?"

A Swiss blade appeared in Branson's hand. Instead of going around to cut him loose, he wrapped his arms around Svenni in a lover's embrace. Svenni held his breath, staring straight at the strong chin and tempting throat. Why did this man affect him like none other?

"A warning device that the flash bomb in the trunk has been activated," Branson murmured, as he worked the blade with a quick swish. He didn't move away. "They'd watched me secure my briefcase inside before I came in here. They must have gotten bored when I didn't come out."

"Let me get this straight," Svenni said, still refusing to look up. "You planted a bomb in your car because you thought someone would steal your briefcase. Doesn't that also mean your briefcase of important stuff just went kaboom too?"

He watched in fascination at Branson's Adam's apple moving before hearing a soft chuckle above him.

"Only if the briefcase had any important stuff. It was just a flash bomb, the kind that doesn't go kaboom. Mostly fire and the element of surprise. The gunfire was just the stupid idiots' reacting to one of their own screaming and I wouldn't be surprised if Dimitri's men didn't start shooting at them after that. I suppose that's what you'd call my backup system."

If not for the urgency in the air, they could have been slow-dancing. Svenni felt the hands gliding down his ass in a slow caress. They cupped his cheeks, squeezing intimately. Then Branson's towering body lowered down and Svenni couldn't move as he watched the big guy knelt down before him. Those warm hands traveled down his thighs.

The windows rattled irritably as gunfire continued. But all he cared about was Branson's face inches from his crotch. His free hands were still numbed or he'd pull that dark head a lot closer.

Branson looked up, his knowing eyes mocking. His hands tickled the back of Svenni's knees.

"Actually, there are three choices," he said, still in that soft tone.

"You're mad if you think we have time to do that right now," Svenni told him, his voice equally hushed.

Branson sighed. "You're right. A kiss then, to convince you to choose to come with me."

As always, his words were loaded with meaning. Branson's head dipped towards Svenni's telltale bulge. A quick nibble and suck.

Svenni swore. His cock was a slave to this man.

Then Branson was standing before him again. "Let's go," he said.

He hadn't even felt his shoes being untied. Svenni swore again.

"I thought you said we didn't have time for that," Branson reminded him.

Poisoned Pawn. *A Pawn (often White's Pawn on b2) which is left as an open target to lure the opponent but is often a trap. When taken, the player who gave up the Pawn can later engage in a strong attack to win the piece taking the Pawn.*

CHAPTER THREE

Martin Branson wanted to shut out the world and take what he wanted. Only the need to protect the man in his charge stopped him from being selfish.

Self control, where are you?

Put all the blame on three years of needing a long cold drink on a hot day named Svenni Jorgensen. And not getting it.

Just his luck. Now he was free to please himself and the man he'd planned for a leisurely chase for so long was also a wanted man by other bad guys. Always so damned inconvenient.

Martin Branson had known what he'd wanted the very first time he'd set eyes on Svenni in a room full of treasure reps, curio-hunters, secret bidders and underground marketers. The bright golden hair, straight, with a short pageboy cut that would look too feminine on a slighter man, but on a tall man, it only served as a focal point for any roving eye. And yes, it'd certainly caught his attention.

He'd taken note of the attractive build and had moved on, doing his job, looking for familiar faces he'd memorized from file photos who would be present at such events.

Then the blond head had turned around.

Wide set eyes, straight nose, and a pair of lips asking to be kissed. A stubborn jaw too. Before he could stop himself, Martin had taken a few steps toward the figure, wanting to be nearer.

He had to stop himself. How inconvenient. He was there on a first outing with Margaret Wyman and he was supposed to slowly let her see his interest in her. He couldn't go off chasing after strange handsome young men who caught his eye right then. So he'd forced himself to turn his attention back to the woman beside him and made an extra effort to engage her in conversation other than business.

His new game—what they called each new mission in his corporation—had started. This was going to be a long one. Getting Miss Wyman's trust was no easy feat. He'd signed on because he'd wanted to see what it was like in a long term game, instead of the usual hunt-and-return quests in which Knights, Inc., specialized. He'd experienced the mercenary side, going after thieves and capturing and returning treasures. Hunting down other mercenaries had been fun, reminding him of his spec. op. days. Locating weapon caches in remote places for some governments had been interesting assignments. He'd never been interested in Knights, Inc.'s internal politics until he was approached by his commander and someone higher up for this assignment. After he'd listened to the assignment details, he'd thought about it and signed on. A long commission but once the game was completed, the rewards would be great, a promotion including a long paid-for vacation.

He saw the young man again a few weeks later and this time they were introduced. Those bright blue eyes fanned by blond eyelashes had studied him, looking for signs, but Martin had had years of keeping his bi-sexual leanings a secret, courtesy of the army, and knew the other man would find nothing.

He'd quietly cursed again at the bad timing. Damned inconvenient. He couldn't afford to make a move now that Margaret was interested in him. There would be no secret dates with another man because she had eyes everywhere.

He hadn't known then the assignment would last almost three years. The woman was tougher than he'd first thought, her security very tight, her secrets well-guarded. It took a long time to gain enough of her trust to even handle some of her business as a pretense of using his Knights, Inc. influence. Meanwhile, a few other people had been murdered and he was determined to do his job and stop Margaret and her connections from killing more.

And there was Mr. Svenni Jorgensen torturing him with those baby blues all that time. Thank God they hadn't bumped into each other often, but when they did, the younger man had never been able to hide his attraction either, always teasing and mocking him. The air sizzled whenever they were together, Svenni's unspoken attraction drew him like a magnet. It took all his army training to resist, to always act as if nothing was happening. It was then he realized his casual indifference turned Svenni on even more, that he liked being controlled by a bigger man. If there were any sexual encounters in the future—and Martin had hoped there would be—he knew what it'd take to have the handsome man for his own. He'd been incredibly aroused—and frustrated—by the knowledge.

And now, finally, Martin had had a taste of handsome, capricious, smart-mouthed Svenni Jorgensen. He wanted more. He couldn't keep his hands off his new lover, even when bullets were flying nearby. Indeed, three years of biding his time had made him into a reckless, lust-blinded fool.

"Jesus, Branson, you pick a fine time to have fun, don't you? Fine, I'll come with you, but you better have a solid plan of escape other than brandishing the broomstick I suggested," Svenni said.

Martin hid a smile. He loved that smart-mouth. And so, so reckless all the time, heedlessly flirting and antagonistic at the same time, daring everyone to stop his poking fun at everything.

"I do have a few weapons better than a broomstick," he said. "We need a getaway car, though."

"I have a vehicle parked nearby. I assume we're going to run for it."

"Unless you have an invisible cloak, I'm afraid we'll have to get a bit dirty."

Svenni snorted. "Do you have more than one gun or do I have to hide behind that big broad back of yours for protection?"

Martin grinned. He handed over a Walther PPK. "Hope you're good at it. If not, just aim and pull the trigger."

There was another snort as the younger man checked the weapon. "My car is closer to the back exit."

"We'll take the fire escape," Martin said, pulling out his Glock and heading for the door.

The hallway was empty. If there had been anyone up there this early, they were long gone or hiding under the beds. Martin moved on, ignoring the sounds downstairs as he made sure there weren't any enemies lurking in the shadows.

"Familiar with this place, aren't you?"

"Hmmm." Dimitri was a friend from the army days. "We're going through that window."

Martin went first. Looking down on the alley, he studied the bar's back entrance.

"Clear." He beckoned to Svenni. "It won't take them long to regroup out front. When they've gathered their wits, they'll think of coming back here."

His long strides took four or five steps at a time. His companion followed nimbly. Jumping over the last railing, he turned around to watch Svenni doing the same, admiring the graceful way he easily landed on his feet. The guy *was* once a professional thief, after all.

Martin started to head out of the alley when Svenni tapped him on the shoulder. He glanced back inquiringly.

"Excuse me. Do you know where my car is?" Svenni asked, polite as could be.

Martin hesitated. Then he gave a half-shrug and ceded his lead. What could he say, he was used to taking charge.

"Yeah, thought so," Svenni said and took over point. He bolted off down one way like a gazelle, calling over his shoulder. "Try to keep up, big guy."

Just then a car pulled in from behind them.

Martin looked back. The driver must have caught sight of them at the same moment. The car's tires skidded and smoked as it suddenly sped up. He saw weapons popping out of the windows.

"Look out!" Martin yelled and dove behind a brick divider.

Checking on Svenni, he saw the younger man peering out of a recessed archway, weapon ready. Grimly, he turned back and started firing his gun at the speeding car. He aimed for the windshield. Taking out the driver was their only chance.

Bullets zinged down the alley. The acrid smell of gunpowder and smoke wafted through. One of his bullets or Svenni's found the target. The car swerved left and crashed into a big dumpster. Men poured out of one side of the vehicle. Martin methodically started to pick them off one at a time. Something whizzed by close enough to hurt but he kept his hand steady, focusing on his assailants. One went down but the others used the car doors for protection.

He counted five. The driver's top half hung out through the windshield, over the hood, bleeding like a pig.

The back door to Dimitri's bar swung open and the volume of weapons firing ratcheted up to ear-piercing levels as the thick walls echoed every round. Martin looked at Svenni's direction and was relieved to find him unhurt, in a crouched position and taking shots. Svenni signaled an OK. He signaled back, making a cutting motion across his throat, then gesturing to keep going as planned. No need to continue. Let Dimitri and his men take care of what was left of their assailants.

Svenni made an OK sign again and went for it, his long legs making his run look effortless. His golden locks bobbed up and down and while he followed him, Martin grinned at the incongruous image of Svenni as a nymph being chased down. Which made him the chaser. Yeah, nice fantasy but as usual, the little fucker had a way of inconveniently distracting him when he should be giving his full attention to *other* things. A stray bullet hit a garbage can a few feet away. Such as not getting killed, Branson, would be good.

Svenni had rounded the corner just as Martin heard shouts from behind. He glanced back to see a few men scuffling on the ground. He thought he caught sight of Dimitri's figure looking towards him. Turning the same side of the alley where Svenni had gone, he didn't bother to continue checking what was happening back there. He could see a small parking area and Svenni.

Dimitri's men would win that fight, no doubt in his mind, and the question left was whether he'd keep one alive for questioning. He hoped not. He'd prefer for D. to think it was just a regular gang fight, even though it was a bit early in the day. Already, he could hear the sirens. That ought to keep everyone busy for a while.

Svenni stood by a car, waiting for him. "You've been shot," he said, his blue eyes looking him up and down.

Remembering a sting somewhere in the shoulder, Martin had thought so but adrenaline was keeping any pain away. "Let's go," he said, reaching for the door. No time to think about wounds.

Svenni got in on the driver's side. The radio blared some stupid rock song. A minute later, they were down the main drag. A speeding police car passed them on the other side.

"How badly hurt?" Svenni asked.

"Don't know. Go, go, go," Martin ordered.

"I'm just worried you'll mess my seat up, that's all." A moment later, he added, "Does it hurt?"

"I can't hear you. The radio is too loud," Martin replied. "Go faster. Let's get out of the main road."

"Son-of-a-bitch. Always have to be in control."

Martin gave Svenni a long look. The younger man returned his gaze for a few moments before giving the road his attention. His face was flushed. Martin sat back and tried to ignore the pounding in his upper shoulder. He willed himself to relax to slow down the bleeding. He looked out the window.

"Where are you taking us?"

"No fucking idea. Where were *you* taking me—the airport?"

"It's a private strip. We aren't scheduled yet."

Svenni frowned at him. "Fine, so we can't go there and the hospital is out of the question."

"Where were you heading after Tallinn?" Martin asked. He hadn't been able to figure out why Svenni flew to Estonia, of all places. Sure, the data miner, Konstantin, was very good but there were other ways to transfer files. "Selling that flash drive would take at least a few days. I traced your credit card to a hotel here but you booked for just one night."

"You fucking put a trace on my credit card?" Svenni yelled over the music.

Martin shrugged. "You do something stupid, you get caught."

"It wasn't stupid. I told everyone I was flying to Estonia to check out some old maps. I wasn't expecting someone kidnapping me."

"You're driving the kidnapper right now and he's asking you where you're taking him," Martin reminded him patiently.

"Only because you're...dammit...bleeding all over my car!" Svenni reached back and pulled a towel from behind his seat. "Here. I was going to take the ferry to Helsinki but that idea is out the window now. Can't do that and not have everyone wondering about the dying man hanging on my arm."

"I'm not dying," Martin told him mildly. He didn't think the bullet was lodged in his arm. "Why Helsinki?"

"Hello. Jorgensen is my last name."

Martin thought about it a moment. "Family."

"So damn brilliant. You should be in MENSA."

It amused him Svenni was getting so comfortable with him, he didn't notice they were actually arguing. Their former conversations had been polite ping-pong in comparison. Except when Svenni would bait him with some sly remark. He had always wondered what it would be like if he'd given in to the sexual tension.

"It could be you have someone else you wanted to see," Martin pointed out. "But then if you do have someone special, you didn't seem to be in a hurry, stopping at a bar for a quickie."

Svenni sneered at him. "I wasn't looking for one—just wanted to drink and relax. Your powers of deduction seemed to not take into consideration I was there too early for some real action. If there had been the usual crowd, you wouldn't have gotten me so easily, Branson."

"Martin," Martin corrected. "Yes, I wondered about that. Thought you were feeling lonely and needed company."

That earned him a laugh. He watched Svenni's profile, fascinated with the crinkle from the corner of his eye and the attractive slash at the side of that sweet mouth. He could see that mouth coming down on him and....

"Are you done making fun of me? You've done that all fucking day. Seriously, I've never seen you so damn casual with me before. It's..." Svenni looked at him again. "...nice. But a bit unsettling. I'm thinking I could get to like it, except for the 'want to force me to go to India and see your boss' bit. I take it you haven't changed your mind, even though I'm driving us somewhere."

"Nope, you're still mine to take," Martin told him, and, in spite of the growing discomfort of his tightening muscle, laughed at Svenni's expression. "I'm not done with you yet."

Damn, it was wonderful to be free again. It felt so good to be able to tease someone he wanted.

"So, Estonia is a way to cover your tracks about visiting family in Finland," he mused. "Sorry you're going to miss seeing them this time round."

Svenni shrugged. "I'll call Nunu. My sister. A musician. Two kids. Any other questions?"

Not about your sister. About you. And me. "Anything about me you need to know that isn't in that file of yours?"

"Konstantin was very thorough."

"But he didn't find out about my romantic preferences." Martin checked the side mirror one last time. Satisfied they weren't being followed, he leaned back and stretched his legs. "Not a big surprise. I'm very good at secrets."

"And acting. I...did you like Margaret Wyman? Because I've always thought there was no chemistry between you two. You were like arm candy for her."

It'd taken all his patience and training to keep his act so long. Among his friends and peers, his self-control had been legendary and he could count on his fingers the few close friends who knew some of his secrets. "It started slowly," Martin explained, knowing how it all looked to the other man. "She was very careful and I had to be extra vigilant about who and what I was. We chose not to lie about my background too much—a Knights, Inc. man would be of interest to her, anyway. I could clue her in about treasure hunts in casual conversation and if we became intimate, there could be more valuable information she could divulge."

"And of course, intimacy was the goal."

"Yes." He looked at Svenni. "She was in cahoots to assassinate certain people and my job was to find out who, why, and hopefully, stop her. I didn't succeed in two cases but got to the third one in time."

There was a short silence as he waited for Svenni to digest his story. Assassinations weren't a normal topic of conversation but he was a former spy and Svenni, a former thief. Their world of treasure hunting was full of people with odd careers. No, he understood Svenni's probing was more about his relationship with Margaret.

"So, the breaking up part was a real break up," Svenni finally said.

"Real enough that she's behind bars," Martin said. He'd conveniently broken off their relationship when he "discovered" papers she'd stolen from him just before the authorities showed up at her gated home, armed with evidence of illegal activities. "Not for the murders which my boss sent me to prevent, unfortunately. That had to stay on the quiet side since they involved our own dealings, but I've found out Margaret had a way of making certain competition disappear."

"I gather there is no making up or second chances in this romance?"

Martin closed his eyes, relaxing into his seat. "Nope. So where are you taking us on our first date?"

There was another brief silence. He felt Svenni's gaze on him but didn't open his eyes. He'd wondered whether the other man would run as soon as he was freed and was pleasantly surprised he hadn't. Maybe everything would work out the way he'd planned, after all.

"You must be light-headed from loss of blood," Svenni interrupted his reverie. "I don't recall you asking for one. Besides, bleeding to death isn't good dating protocol."

"Shows you how much I really want to be with you," Martin jibed. "Or maybe you just want to dump me out of the car and take off."

"I'm thinking about it. Then I could go catch my ferry ride to Helsinki and see my sister, like I'd planned."

"I feel used and abused." Martin smiled at the short burst of curses filling the air. "Okay, that one time with your butt straight up the air was me doing the using and abusing. If you could turn down the music and the shouting? My head hurts."

To his relief, the music stopped.

"Happy now?"

"Thank God. I need to educate you on good music. And better ways to use that filthy mouth of yours."

"Martin, I'm going to kill you in bed."

"But I'm dying, remember?"

He smiled again as he drifted off. Svenni had called him Martin.

PROTECTED PASSED PAWN. *A Pawn protected defensively by another pawn.*

CHAPTER FOUR

Svenni parked the car under the torn awning and took out his cell phone from his pocket. He punched the number from memory. It rang three times before the familiar hoarse voice picked up.

"It's me," he said. "Is it okay to bring a guest in? Injured."

"How long will you be staying?"

"Not long. I need to look at his wound and clean him up."

"All right. Come on in." The line went dead.

"Who was that?" Branson asked, looking out the window.

"We're at a friend's place. It's safe. Do you need help getting out?"

"I'm fine."

Svenni snorted. "Yeah, yeah, flesh wound, barely a scratch, etcetera, Sir Knight. Let's go in before you pass out and then I'd have to carry you."

He didn't show his worry but Martin looked pale and although the bleeding had stopped, the soaked towel evidenced the seriousness of his injury. He imagined that shoulder must be throbbing by now, even though his passenger hadn't said anything during the two hour trip.

"Are you sure you aren't dying?" he asked now, as a way to voice his concern.

Branson got out of the car and quietly shut the door. "My dying would kind of put a damper to our date," he said with a slight smile.

Svenni glanced heavenward as if looking for help there, then opened the back door to get some of his stuff. He hoped unexpectedly bringing Branson here wouldn't cause too much trouble for his friend but this was an emergency, no matter how nonchalant the guy was about his injury.

They went round back and up the porch steps. After rapping a few times, there was a click. The door opened and a familiar face peered out.

"Sven."

"Jaan, sorry about this."

"Eh, you're always trouble." The door swung wider. "Come on in."

Svenni grinned fondly at the older figure. It'd been a year or so since he'd visited his mentor and it felt good to see him looking well. He jerked his head at Branson to follow him as he entered the house.

"This is Branson, a friend, and..."

"And he's hurt," Jaan interrupted, his gaze on Branson's wound. "Introductions and explanation later. You get him upstairs and fix that. I'll get the emergency kit. Lock the door behind you. Make sure you bring the medication case up by the stairwell."

"Yes, sir," Svenni said meekly as he did what he was told.

He found the small box on the table next to the stairs. Branson was right behind him, still silent. He turned and pointed to the lowered ceiling near the first landing.

"Watch out for that," he said. "I've hit my head many a time while climbing up these steps in the dark."

"Did you live here?"

"Sometimes." It was home. Sort of. "Jaan likes his privacy, though, so I don't come too often. My room is to your left."

Branson lifted one dark eyebrow. "*Your* room."

Damn it. Slip of tongue. "Guest room," he corrected smoothly as he reached out to push the door open. "Come on. Jaan is going to be up here any minute to take a look at that hole in your shoulder."

"Is he a doctor?"

"Not really."

"So are you sure he knows what he's doing?"

"Well, he's pretty good at stitching up parchments," Svenni said glibly. "What do you want, a hospital? A private doctor who actually knows about gunshots? This is the next best thing."

Branson sat down on the bed and looked around. "When they ask me what I saw in Estonia, I'm going to tell them bedrooms. Nice pic of you and Jaan in the *guest* room."

Svenni sighed. "It's not what you're thinking and I don't think I need to explain anything to you, buddy."

"Did I say anything?"

Svenni jabbed him lightly with a finger. "Don't ask Jaan any questions either when he comes up. Now let's take off that shirt and let me see." He ignored the glint in those sexy dark eyes as he bent over, pulling the stained shirt up slowly. Detecting a slight narrowing around the other man's eyes, he stopped, cocking his head.

"I'm good," Branson assured him, stiffly lifting the arm.

"Your eye twitched. Probably easier to cut this off you."

"Now you're scaring me. You can read my eye twitches."

True. That was a bit scary, but Svenni was learning how much control the man had over his emotions. One had to watch Mr. Tall, Dark, and Expressionless like a hawk to get any feedback. He took a pair of scissors out of his backpack and gestured. Branson stretched the material for easier access and soon there were pieces of shirt everywhere.

The wound, near the fleshy part of the shoulder, looked like a misshapen fish mouth, purplish-red and swollen. It was still bleeding lightly. Dry blood caked one side of the muscular chest. Oh yeah, dude had to be in pain.

"Close by the armpit," Svenni murmured, examining it without touching. "Are you sure...okay, I see the burnt marks. The bullet must have barely grazed you. Very close call."

"Told you it was nothing."

"It doesn't mean there's no shrapnel inside. It needs to be cleaned."

"Pour lots of alcohol on it."

"Want some painkillers?" Svenni opened up the small meds box. "These are good stuff here."

"None of that for me, thanks." Branson said. "Just get me a bottle of brandy or something."

"I don't think they're addictive," Svenni said, pulling out a bottle. "Take two. The cleaning is going to take some time."

Frowning, Branson shook his head, then tempered his obstinacy with a devastating smile. "You might take advantage of me or something."

Bloody chest with gaping wound or not, that smile had the effect of giving Svenni lots of sexy ideas about playing doctor and patient. That tan skin. The flat stomach. The light pelt on the chest that intriguingly disappeared into the pants.

A light knock at the door interrupted his slow perusal.

"Ready?" Jaan asked as he folded his sleeves.

"Ah...ahem. Yeah, but he doesn't want any meds. Just brandy," Svenni replied. He needed to down a strong drink too. "And we're going to need to clean that wound."

His old mentor had worked as a medic during wartime. He was quiet as he assessed the injury, his hands steady as they were with fragile documents. He probed the opening with a finger. Branson growled.

"Steady," Jaan murmured.

"How about that drink first?" Branson asked in a strained voice.

"I'll get it," Svenni said, not wanting to watch any more. He wasn't squeamish but fingers inside open gaping bloody flesh? Nope. "Be right back."

When he returned, Branson had a white ring around his mouth and he was breathing harshly. He quickly strode over and offered the bottle of brandy he'd found in the cabinet. The big man accepted it with his free hand and without a single word, chugged down several big gulps.

"That must mean you're hurting," Svenni commented softly.

Branson kept the bottle by his side. The white of his eyes were tinged pink. "Didn't even say ouch," he jibed back just as softly, his breathing still a bit erratic.

"He has a strong tolerance for pain," Jaan agreed as he picked up a basin. "We're going to clean that wound with alcohol now. Going to sting just a little."

"So he's going to be okay?" Svenni asked.

"Got out some bullet bits. Just need some stitches. Basically, a flesh wound."

"Told ya," Branson said, getting up when Jaan beckoned him to follow.

"So disappointed. Thought I had to hold you down for some old-fashion amputation. Then you can be the One-Armed Kidnapper."

"Kidnapper?" Jaan asked, his eyebrows raised. "You drove your kidnapper here?"

"Long story," Svenni answered.

"He exaggerates a lot," Branson said. "Ever since I've met him, he's always telling tall tales about me and him hunting for treasure."

Jaan chuckled. "Tall tales. Your friend has a sense of humor."

The three of them were in a small bathroom, dwarfing it even more. Branson leaned over the tub. Jaan shook his head.

"That's not going to work. You need to get into the tub or the place is going to get wet."

"Better take off your pants," Svenni added smugly. "We don't have another pair that big."

See how he liked being at a disadvantage now.

* * *

Svenni took a last gulp of his own drink. Needed it. And maybe a cold shower.

He ran a hand through his hair. The last hour had been a test of his willpower. Fucking guy nonchalantly dropped his pants and he was all commando. *Of course*! Why would he not be? And he stood there, in the tub, a six-foot-five statue of masculine beauty, corded powerful arms and legs, the trailing chest hair that had tempted him before that—Svenni shook his empty bottle, wishing for another swallow—narrowed down to the dark pelt between those legs. And a tattoo on that tight ass. The dried blood smears only made the sight even more sensuous, like he was a god of war after a battle just arriving home to be cleaned off.

Damn it all to hell. How was he going to ever fantasize again without thinking about that hard body? Clean it off indeed. He had to make sure his tongue wasn't lolling out of his mouth the whole time they were in the bathroom. After pouring all the alcohol over the wound and watching the liquid form rivulets down that chest, body and the *rest* of Branson, he'd felt like volunteering for drying duty. With his own tongue.

"He's going to be in a bad temper when he comes to and realizes you spiked his brandy," Jaan said from the kitchen table in the corner.

Svenni shrugged. He laid the empty bottle of alcohol in the sink and poured away the rest of the brandy. He'd wanted Branson to rest and had a feeling the guy wasn't going to, especially with a painful throb in his shoulder. He'd associated with special forces types before and they tended to be control freaks even when they were injured. Besides, it would give him some time to talk to Jaan without Branson breathing down his neck and distracting him. He figured he could deal with the bad temper side when the time came.

"The sedative isn't very strong. It'd probably just relaxed him enough for him to take the nap he desperately needs."

"So you're now no longer his kidnappee?"

Svenni grinned at the mild amusement in his mentor's voice. "I've always been good at getting away," he said, as he put a kettle on the stove. "I'm tired too and wanted to talk to you without needing to go round and round a topic. He's a smart dude and will start sniffing around if he thought you were of use to him."

"Interesting. Yet you brought him here."

Svenni shrugged again. It seemed the best option at that time.

"So, Branson what's the rest of his name?"

"Martin Branson, actually. American, if you can't tell from his accent. I've known him for a while now but mostly as an acquaintance." He ignored Jaan's small smile. "Earlier today, he appeared out of nowhere and...took me by surprise."

Jaan regarded him for a moment. His eyebrows slowly went up, deepening the vertical wrinkles on his high forehead. "You can leave him here and take off. I won't let him come after you."

And leave that hot body behind? No way in fucking hell. That naked man upstairs is all mine. Svenni coughed, hoping his face didn't betray his thoughts.

"He was taking me to meet his boss in India. I want to go find out what this is all about so there's no point running off. His people know a lot about me so perhaps they know about you too. He's with Knights, Inc., a corporation of treasure-hunters-for-hire."

"A dummy corporation," Jaan corrected, taking a sip from his tea. "They've been around for a while."

"You know about them?" Svenni asked, surprised. Once Jaan had retired, he'd shown no indication of keeping his ear to the underground grapevine. This must be an old organization. "You never mentioned them."

"They're secretive. Not easy to dig anything beyond the dummy corporations they set up through the years. I do know a bit, though, because I've dealt with them once or twice. Knights, Inc. is a business subsidiary of The Temple. It has a long history of mixing treasure hunting and spying, and rumored to be founded by a group of Templar knights on the run from King Philip of France."

Svenni blinked. Whoa. And here he'd spent a fortune buying information from Konstantin when he could have had all the details from his own mentor. Seven years on his own had made him forget his own roots. Jaan Kinnunen was a historian and archaeology assistant before the many civil wars around Eastern Europe had changed him into a master thief, before he rescued a young punk on the run from a group of policemen in Egypt.

The kettle whistled softly. He turned the stove off and took a cup dangling off a hook under the cabinet.

"Want more tea?" he asked. "Remember my run-in with Dante a long time ago?"

Jaan held out his cup for some of the hot water. "Of course. Your injuries were extensive."

Svenni pushed away that particular unpleasant memory. "These Knights people are dealing with him and a treasure map. And Branson told me Dante has put a price out on me. He's hurt partly because Dante's men were shooting at us."

Jaan blew on his tea, his expression thoughtful. "Why do you think he's after you?"

"It has to do with that map I tried to steal."

"But that was—eight? Nine? Years ago. How is it connected?"

He had been very young and too brash. The job had been beyond his capabilities and he'd never forgotten that particular lesson because of what he'd gone through and seen after being caught by Dante. Sometimes, hearing the normal sound of a child screaming would awaken that distant memory again, accompanied by cold sweats and goose bumps.

"I'm not sure but this was what Branson showed me," Svenni said, finally sitting down at the table. He pulled out the small odd-shaped object and set it on the table. "I haven't a clue what this thing is but those symbols are the same ones I memorized from that treasure map. I don't know why Dante is after me but Branson and company seems to think it has to do with the fact I tried to steal the map long ago. Can't connect all the dots, so I'm going to India."

His mentor palmed the artifact gently, weighing it. "This is an old replica. Still valuable because of its age, but a fake," he said. "Branson's boss probably has the real thing locked up in The Temple."

"There is really a place called The Temple?" Svenni asked. "These people are sounding weirder and weirder."

"Imagine a centuries old tradition," Jaan said, putting down the carved object. "The players called it The Game. Every game is high risk, high stakes, and only the richest and most powerful get to play."

Svenni stared at Jaan. The whole idea sounded ridiculous; yet, the world of treasures had always been murky. "Are you saying they're playing a game that lasted for centuries?"

"No, they had different games. Some not so big as others. As time went by, they included spying for different governments, getting weaponry, hostage exchanges, that sort of thing, as part of their retinue, but treasure hunting is their foundation. That's what those Templar Knights were infamous for, you know, keeping treasures. The Temple has evolved to keep up with the times. Nowadays governments have so much say on who owns which treasure and stolen artifacts get into the news so much quicker that the Game had gotten tougher. By dipping in certain helpful spy 'games,' and thus exchanging political favors, they get the authorities to turn a blind eye to The Temple's main mission, keeping The Game going."

"I need something stronger," Svenni muttered. He stood up and opened the liquor cabinet. He came back with a bottle and poured liberally into his cup of tea. "Branson said they call themselves 'knights.' I thought he was kidding. Now I find out he's part of a medieval game of some kind that involves temples and treasures and worse, that monster Dante."

"But you still like this fellow and still want to go with him," Jaan pointed out.

Svenni finished his tea. "Jaan, there's something about him I really, really like."

"Besides that sculpted naked body, you mean?"

Svenni grinned raffishly. "There is that. Speaking of which, I'd better go upstairs to make sure he isn't awake. Have to put this back before he finds out."

"Get some food from the fridge. He told me while I was stitching him up you guys only had some energy bars during the ride. You eat first then take with you some food and orange juice for the blood loss. Careful with my stitches, please. Nothing too energetic."

Svenni's grin widened at the indulgent look on his mentor's face. "Jaan, I'm just going to shower and go to bed."

"Just giving medical advice, that's all. It's not everyday I see my boy look so happy being kidnapped. Be careful, Sven. I have a bad feeling about this game."

Svenni nodded. "Yeah, me too. Better to stick by the big guy and find out more."

"I'm sure you won't find that a hardship," Jaan said wryly and hid his face behind his cup.

* * *

Svenni had quietly left the tray of food on the night table and slipped into the bathroom, trying not to make too much noise. After a quick hot shower, he wrapped a towel around his waist and stepped back in the room. His gaze immediately went to the sleeping man on the bed. He froze. And all thought of sleep vanished.

Branson was no longer asleep. It appeared he ate his meal while waiting for him to emerge from the bathroom.

It was difficult to imagine a sexier calendar pose than what was presented in front of him. In his usually boring bed was a naked man, barely-covered by rumpled sheets, hand resting on a knee. The intensity in those dark, dark eyes tightened Svenni's gut and made his towel shift.

In fact, in spite of that empty plate saying otherwise, Branson still looked mighty hungry. One corner of those sensual lips lifted. The hand lifted and a finger beckoned, daring him to come closer.

Oh, he dared. This man was his tonight.

Svenni sauntered slowly toward his target. "You look better," he said. More than better. He inspired erotic fantasies. "Even drank the juice like a good boy."

"Alcohol and drugs usually make one thirsty," Branson said very softly.

"It was only a very mild sedative. I wanted you to rest and pain doesn't help one to fall asleep," Svenni retorted. "How's the pain level now?"

"Tolerable. Trying to feed me more drugs?" Branson reached out and pulled on the knot keeping his towel in place. "I have other ways to distract me."

"I was told to be careful with your stitches," Svenni murmured, his heart thudding faster as the towel dropped to the floor. "You can't move too much."

"Do you have any plans? Besides drugging me and searching my pockets?"

Svenni glanced up sharply. Branson's gaze was on his dick, his hand gently and persistently moving up and down. "I think you—" His words came out in a guttural mix when the big hand enclosed around his cock tugged and he was pulled closer. The other hand gathered and massaged his balls, one long finger teasing the crack of his ass.

"Still thinking?" Branson asked.

"No," he managed to say, "but careful...your stitches..."

"Then you mustn't fight rough like you did earlier today."

Had it only been one day? It seemed as if they'd been at this sexual match for a long, long time.

"I didn't put up such a fight."

Branson smiled. "Get in bed before I tackle you in here."

As if he needed a second invitation. Svenni pulled off the tempting covers. Holy hotdog. He studied the beautiful sight of the big and handsome cock standing at attention. His fingers itched with the need to touch. Not taking his eyes off, he climbed into bed.

Branson's hand on his own erection tugged him closer. Even closer. Svenni scooted over the big tan body, one knee on each side. Their cocks touched, velvet steel swords crossing and teasing each other. He undulated against the rock hard heat, fascinated by his uncut penis thudding against the huge circumcised pole growing from the nest of dark hair. His own cock's head was already plenty damp with pre-come.

He reached down and rubbed his juice all over Branson's penis. The feel of the smooth marble-hard length turned him on even more. That was inside him today, that whole hot towering inferno. More pre-come leaked out of him and he oiled the object of his desire lovingly with it.

Branson unexpectedly brought up a hand behind his neck, insistently pulling Svenni in for his kiss. His mouth was warm and his lips firm. Svenni opened his and Branson's tongue invaded with a passion that sent a sizzling need right down his spine into his ass.

The man's kiss was slow and addictive, exploring his tongue and mouth in lazy possession, and he responded automatically, his arms wrapping around the broad back. He didn't kiss a lot. It wasn't a thing many of his past lovers were into. But the lips moving against his made him want to do this forever.

It was such a powerful seduction, he barely acknowledged the hands on his waist and in one smooth move, his back was on the soft bed and that big hot body was on top, that sexy mouth still capturing his, the tongue drinking his whole soul. Owning it.

When Branson's lips released him, he stared up into those fathomless dark eyes, wondering what went on in there, whether the other man felt the same urgency he did. His need to be taken by Branson scared him. Had he ever wanted another so much?

"My hot blue-eyed blond Scandinavian," Branson whispered. "Open your legs and let me fuck you."

Svenni did as he was told.

Time stood still as their movements became slow and deliberate. Branson's magnificent body leaned over, his good shoulder trapping his with his weight as he used his other hand to position his erection. Svenni opened wider, helping him. He gasped in sheer delight at the sensual burn as Branson slowly pushed inside. He watched as the bigger man balanced himself on one arm.

Those dark eyes had a wicked, wicked look in them.

"One-armed bandit, did you request?" he asked.

Svenni's eyes rounded as Branson then proceeded to fuck him doing one armed push-ups. His other hand, with the injured shoulder, wrapped around his neck, letting him know who was boss here.

"Don't look away. I want to see you come as I fill your ass with mine," Branson said, his voice velvety seductive. "I want to see those baby blues glaze over and give me that sexy surrender. Give me what I want or I won't fuck you. Suck you. Take you every way possible tonight."

Just those words made Svenni come close to coming but he held back, wanting to prolong the pleasure. He gazed into the other man's eyes. He pushed his hips up, meeting thrust for slow thrust, angling this way and that to get that mind-tingling slide against his prostate.

"I'll suck you till the rest of what's left of your blood rushes to your cock," Svenni promised, his voice barely a hoarse gasp. "And then I'll suck you dry."

"Only if you surrender right now. Look at me. Give it, give it, give it."

And Svenni gave. And gave. And gave. His orgasm streamed out in pure heated ecstasy, splattering on the other man's tanned skin. And he was lost in Branson's gaze, which held him prisoner as he went under. There was nothing but Branson, the feel of him, the touch, the scent, the very essence. He held on to the muscular arms tightly, lifting his hips higher. Harder.

The world was a dark night filled with myriads of shooting stars, each landing somewhere between his balls and penis and exploding into a thousand shuddering delights. He heard Branson's now familiar deep-throated groan and the heavy body fell against him as the big guy shook in his arms.

When he came to, his face was buried in Branson's chest, the scent of sexy man sweat and sex in his nose. He sleepily inhaled in deep appreciation. Ah, he'd been hounded by this guy's scent forever. Needed to find a way to bottle it.

"Round One to the One-Armed Bandit," he heard Branson whisper in his ear before a tongue delved deep and started another seductive assault.

CHAPTER FIVE

Out of habit, Martin woke up without opening his eyes. It was something he'd learned when he was in Special Forces. One never knew what woke one up—normal movement of comrades or the rustle of an enemy walking by. The few seconds to get his head back into reality had saved his life many times.

But this morning's recollection brought forth only most pleasant images of the previous night's activities. He could hear the sleep sounds of his partner beside him, a gentle snuffling and air tickling his neck every few seconds. A warm body snuggled against his—a body perfectly made for him, if he remembered correctly. He allowed a smile to form and opened his eyes

The first thing that always caught his eyes when it came to Svenni was those ridiculously golden locks. No matter how crowded the room, they would catch the light in such a way that Martin never lost awareness of the younger man's whereabouts. It'd been a source of amusement and frustration for him because he wanted to see and talk to Svenni, but couldn't. Shouldn't. There had been lives at stake and any missteps on his part could cost him the game.

At times he'd wondered whether the game was worth it—all the time lost when he could have had Golden Boy in his arms. The little ex-thief, as Margaret had dismissively called him, when she'd investigated his background.

Not so little. His Golden Boy was six foot of glorious strapping man who could steal from him any time, as far as Martin was concerned. But then, things had taken a grim turn. News of one death reached him, and he'd felt like a failure. He hadn't been gathering information from Margaret fast enough to save that person.

All he knew at the time of signing on was someone had decided to target certain important women within his organization. It was only when one of them died that an even higher-up had contacted him and given him the 411. He became privy to a secret about which he wasn't even allowed to discuss with his immediate boss, John Dallas, the CEO of Black Knights, Inc. Keeping Dallas in the dark wasn't something to his liking, but he'd agreed to that because of the assurance that it'd be temporary.

The secret was huge within his organization. The women were candidates chosen as possible replacement for the dying head of the Temple. Targeting them meant someone badly wanted the best of the Temple out of the way. The game was to find out who and why.

Videos and files had shown Margaret Wyman had facilitated the murders. His job was to get close enough to find out why and when. And with the quick nature of the attacks, Martin had no choice.

Golden Boy Svenni Jorgensen would have to wait.

Martin's smile grew. But that wait had certainly paid off handsomely. He was just glad the other man's interest hadn't waned through the years.

Svenni's eyelashes fluttered and his eyes slowly opened, shocking blue slits. His gaze was sleepily sexy.

"Wow. Thought it was just a great dream," he said, and stretched. "Good morning. How's the wound?"

Branson stretched his arm out to examine the stitches. There was a big bruise around the area. "Slightly stiff," he replied. "And you? Any discomfort anywhere?"

It *had* been a long night. His lover's face flushed slightly at his teasing.

"No complaints," he said, and added, "yet."

Branson reached over and traced those sensual lips. The urge to kiss him was overwhelming but if he did that, they'd spend the whole morning in bed.

"There's more if you'd hang around," he said, softly.

"You mean, if I don't get killed off by Dante," Svenni said, his mood shifting slightly.

"I'll protect you. I'm not handing you off to him."

"You said you might yesterday," he pointed out.

Martin raised his brows. "You think, after waiting all these years and finally about to get my vacation, I'll just let you get spirited off by some other man?"

"Hey, I didn't know yesterday, right? Hell, I don't know today what's going on either. Care to fill me in on my immediate future?"

Martin turned onto his back and tucked his good arm under his head. "How much did you find out about Knights, Inc. last night?" He darted Svenni a sideways glance. "I know who he is."

Svenni sniffed. "Is there anything you don't know about me?"

"A lot. I don't know how you feel about spending time with me, for example, after I've gotten you to my boss. A nice vacation where we can be alone and get to talk of things other than an artifact with cuneiform writing on it."

There was a short silence. "That's one hell of a bribe," Svenni remarked.

Martin smiled and wished they could just skip everything and go straight to the vacation part. "I've been told I'm persuasive. Besides, your life's in danger so the quicker we get to the bottom of this, the better."

"I can take care of myself, you know."

"I know."

"I can go so deep into hiding you won't find me for a year, how about that?"

"I know."

"So how come my head is telling me to say yes to you?"

"Because you're smart and because," Branson added smugly, "I turn you on."

He'd known Svenni and he would be hot together, but he didn't want to just have a quick affair and be done with it. In their previous dealings, the younger man was an intriguing combination of sarcastic daredevil, brash and cocky, and yet, with a kind heart.

Once, during a private auction after-party, he'd watched him scale one of the biggest trees at an old estate like it was nothing, just to get the owner's young daughter's yowling cat when a ladder wasn't high enough. It'd been a chaotic event, one of those moments when people who had a few too many were talking too much and yelling up crazy advice. It was fascinating to see Svenni tackling the tree while holding on to a basket and rope as well as talking back at the men below with his usual droll wit. The task of getting to the cat completed, he'd almost fallen off shooing the frightened animal into the basket before covering it up.

Martin remembered his heart stopping for a second at the sight of the lanky body dangling dangerously with no safety net below before Svenni pulled himself up in one smooth move. He'd wondered at that easy strength, had imagined how it would be like to have such a man surrender himself in bed. And would he be as gentle afterwards, as he was with the little girl who hugged him gratefully?

No, he wanted more when it came to Svenni Jorgensen.

"Yeah, you turn me on as much as my ceiling is making you horny," Svenni drawled, as he sat up in bed. "Excuse me, I'll be in the bathroom while you make love to ceiling tiles with your eyes."

Martin quirked his lips. Sarcastic bastard. He watched Svenni's naked ass make a quick retreat. He'd had ample time learning the other man's facial expressions through the years. Svenni was feeling he was letting Branson too close and it was scaring him, so now he was running off to put some space between them.

Nothing wrong with that. He was practically accelerating their relationship the speed of light. He was just going to have to be a bit more patient and let Svenni make up his mind. Meanwhile, he'd better get up too and communicate with his people. He had a feeling there were dangerous times ahead.

* * *

"He has a person inside informing him of your moves. Since I hadn't been compromised in the last three years, the link is through you, not through John or my go-between. I assure you, Margaret would have had me killed. She doesn't have any patience for a long con at all. Dante wouldn't have stopped her either."

Svenni paused in the middle of buttoning his shirt. That name still had a distinct bad taste, one he couldn't forget. Pain was easily forgotten, but the memories from that experience were difficult to shake off. And to think of Branson being caught and maybe at his mercy was a sickening thought.

"No, you aren't pulling me into another game. I didn't sign off on anything. All I did was volunteer my services to pick Jorgensen up and bring him to you because he's a friend of mine. And no, you can't keep him to use as bait after all. Sorry, that part isn't in my vacation plans. You heard right, ma'am. We're going on vacation after you talk to him." Branson's deep drawl during the back-and-forth conversation was matter-of-fact, as if he was reporting to a superior.

Svenni walked in noisily to announce his presence. Branson was standing in the middle of the room, gloriously naked. He looked up and gave a quick smile. He pointed at Svenni's dropped towel from the night before and shrugged.

Ah, his pants were still in the bathroom and of course, his shirt was a useless pile of shredded rags. Damn, maybe he should just keep the man in this state forever. He didn't need a stitch on him.

"Bait?" He mouthed the word as he approached.

Branson shook his head as he kept listening to the voice on the other end. "All true, but again, respectfully, I disagree with your using my man as bait. If you don't have the authority to assure this won't happen, you and John can just continue on without my help. I don't care if you fire me, ma'am. I need that vacation after three years with Margaret. You owe me. I saved your life." He grinned at the response. "Yup, I play dirty when I have to. So, do we have a deal?"

Still listening intently, Svenni went to the dresser and pulled out some shirts from the drawer. He shook them out and picked the largest one. Did he say, 'my man?'

"Time of arrival? Okay. Place and password? Got it. We'll follow the plans unless things changed. Say hi to John and tell him a honeymoon isn't a good time to be in the middle of a game."

Branson laughed, totally at ease with being naked as he accepted the shirt. Svenni so wanted to swat that tight ass.

"Business and pleasure? Nope, those two words don't compute together. It's all pleasure for my vacation, thank you very much." His dark eyes were warm when they held Svenni's questioning gaze.

Svenni watched the play of arm and chest muscles as Branson juggled holding on to a cell phone and donning a shirt at the same time. Pieces of the conversation whirled through his mind. Pawn didn't sound good. The vacation part promised to be sexy but scary. The knowledge that Branson had planned so far ahead about being with him was both exciting and confusing.

To be honest, he felt like running off. Yet strangely, it was even more exciting to know if he did, Branson would just keep chasing. Hell, if he chased him naked like that...Svenni cleared his throat. He must have betrayed his thoughts because there was a wicked gleam in the other man's eyes right now he was beginning to recognize.

"I know he's important," Branson murmured, "more important than you think. I'll be in touch. Goodbye."

His shirt looked good on that big body, molding the chest which he vividly recalled licking every square inch the night before. And then he had moved on downwards....

"Pawn for what?" Svenni demanded, annoyed at his own lack of self-control.

"How about continuing the conversation after I get my pants on?" Branson countered, clapping an arm around Svenni's shoulders for a moment before heading to the bathroom. "Also, something to eat would be nice. I'm starving, aren't you? You need to pack some clothes. Call your sister about not coming to see her this time. I like my coffee black, by the way."

Svenni stared at the empty doorway as sounds of Branson whistling and moving about emerged. There ought to be a ban against cheerful morning people with a list of things to do and who ran around ordering the day to be exactly as they wished. Especially the ones who do it while walking about with no underwear on.

An hour later, they were sitting at the table with Jaan. Jaan had gone through the trouble of making an American breakfast. Svenni cast him a disbelieving look and he shrugged.

"*Pidän hänestä*," Jaan said.

"Well, I do too, but you don't see me making a special breakfast," Svenni said.

"I think my like and your like are two entirely different kinds of like." Jaan laughed and pointed a spoon at Branson, who was enjoying his cup of coffee. "I like him because he plans things and see it through, and planning is very important in our old trade. I think he'd make a good thief...I mean, it's almost like treasure hunting. You also like him for hunting, but again, different kind of like."

Branson laughed quietly.

Svenni scowled. "No fucking idea what you just said. I think I need more coffee," he muttered.

"Eat, make plans, do all kinds of hunting, that's what Jaan's saying," Branson explained, tongue in cheek.

"Yes, exactly," Jaan agreed.

Svenni's scowl deepened. This was getting worse. Jaan liked Branson and would soon be talking about the good old days. It would give the other man even more ammo. Branson knew too damn much about him, as it was.

"Fine," he said out loud. "What's the plan? And how am I the pawn? Why didn't you tell your boss just now what I said about the symbols you showed me? Then we can just skip the India part, you know."

Branson took his time chewing, his gaze resting on Svenni thoughtful and assessing. Jaan didn't seem to mind the small pause as he forked scrambled egg into his mouth. Svenni tapped his fingers on the table, mentally measuring the circumference of Branson's neck and wondering how much pressure it'd take to strangle the man.

Finally Jaan spoke up. "He's never been very patient. Everything must be laid out from beginning to the end."

"I've been upfront about where we're going and how it'll end and yet, more questions," Branson countered. "Can't he just wait till we get to India? Maybe I don't have all the answers."

"My head's on the chopping block. Pardon me if I feel a little nervous," Svenni said wryly. "And now I hear your boss wants to use me as bait and even if you say no, that doesn't mean I can trust your people."

"I need you to trust me," Branson said quietly. "I said I won't let anything happen to you. And I trust these two people I'm taking you to meet. I'd rather they explain the ga...mission to you."

"Game. You wanted to say game, so say it. It's a game to you all."

Branson's eyes shuttered and for the first time since yesterday, his expression reverted to the old Branson Svenni knew, the one who was frustratingly unreadable. "Treasure hunts. Thievery. Stolen artifacts finder. It's all a race to the finish line for the people involved. A game, no matter what you called it. Some make it too personal and lives are risked but you yourself are in it because of the danger. You're part of the game, whether you admit it or not, Svenni. You're an adrenaline junkie, just like the rest of us, more so than me, I suspect, because hey, I didn't go rob Dante with his army of bodyguards all by myself."

Svenni glared at the tall brooding man sitting so close. "Quit bringing up my past. I stopped a long time ago," he asserted, heat creeping into his voice. "I'm a courier now. Of properly bought treasures. If any were stolen, I wouldn't know. They all come with the proper documents for the owners."

Branson's smile was mocking and without thinking, Svenni took a swing at him. His target didn't block but instead dodged just enough that Svenni's fist cuffed only the side of his head.

There was a loud smack and coffee sloshed onto the table.

"Ouch," Branson said, in a mild voice. "I think my stitches broke, Jaan."

Jaan started chuckling, then tried to change it into a cough. He took a quick swallow of his milk, which made him cough. Branson pounded his back.

"I'm okay," Jaan finally said, then took another sip. "I apologize, Sven. That was just too hilarious to watch. I haven't seen you lose your temper in ages."

Svenni picked up his napkin and wiped his mouth. "The guy has ignored me for years and now that he's says 'jump,' I'm supposed to say 'how high?' If it wasn't for your nice stitches, I'd pound him to the ground."

"When he's talking about you but not talking to you, that means he's losing his temper again."

"Ah." Branson refilled his cup. His dark eyes were smiling. "Would it appease him if I tell you the names of the two people we're meeting? That way, it'd show a measure of trust on my part and it'd also give you a means to look for us in case anything happens to us. Will he feel better?"

"I think that would definitely make him less unhappy," Jaan replied, with a smile.

Svenni leaned forward. "It's making *him* feel ganged up on. It's making *him*—" He took a deep breath and exhaled. "—speak of himself in third person, dammit. Quit laughing. All right, all right. I give in. You damn well know your putting your trust in Jaan would put him on your side."

Branson nodded. "Of course. An ally makes every move stronger. Classic battle strategy." He turned to Jaan. "I know you're familiar with The Game and The Temple. The two names to remember are John Dallas and Kel Grant. They're very important players, especially her."

Jaan buttered another piece of bread and popped it into his mouth. He took his time, gray eyes studying Branson. "I know Dallas as the Black Knight. One of the CEO of Knights, Inc., in fact, so he's important. But Kel Grant. Hmm."

"Martin takes orders from her," Svenni told him, "so she must be high up there too."

"Ah. But I know the White Knight, who's a woman, and her name isn't Kel."

"There's a White Knight?" Svenni asked. "Black Knight, White Knight, sounds like a cult of spies."

Jaan smiled. "You're close." He looked at Branson again. "Thank you for your confidence. I'm sure everything will be fine. Sven, I have something for you in my room. First drawer."

Svenni frowned. Jaan wanted him out of the room so he could talk to Branson. Why? Jaan just gave him a small smile.

He stood up, scraping his chair on the tile floor. Fucking fine. He was going to India and then on holiday. Happy, happy, fun, fun.

As he walked out, he heard Jaan said, "He called you Martin."

"I know." Branson's voice was full of smugness.

Svenni swore and trudged upstairs.

The Alekhine Defense. *A provocative strategy of tempting the opposing pawns forward. Black uses his Knight as a target to lure White's Pawns forward so that they become objects of attack*

CHAPTER SIX

They left Jaan's not long after. Martin liked the man and could see Svenni was like a son to him. He gauged him to be around late forties, so the wars in which he was a medic were probably the Balkan wars or any of the civil battles between ethnic groups in East Europe. Martin had had several spec. ops. missions in those countries and had seen some of the bloodiest battles in his experience. Funny. Jaan didn't look like a warfare kind of guy.

Svenni was driving, heading for the highway. The GPS had mapped out the route to the private airstrip near Tallinn.

Martin stretched his legs out and looked at the passing scenery. If things went smoothly, they should be in the air within a few hours.

"What did Jaan say to you?" Svenni asked, interrupting his thoughts.

"What did Jaan have for you upstairs?" Martin countered.

"Gift. None of your business. And don't give me the same reply because it *is* my business if he was talking about me and this game stuff. Your giving him some names doesn't tell me a damn thing about what's going on. I know you deflected a hit on me yesterday and saved my tail but it would be nice to know Dante's intentions."

"We don't know Dante's intentions for you. We have an idea but I'd rather my John and Kel talk to you about it because it isn't my game. That's the point of a game, you know. When you're in it, you play it and make the moves." Martin took a deep breath, trying to find an easy explanation. "In my capacity, my game is done. My quest is completed. I was supposed to collect my rewards, which happened to be you and a certain island holiday, by the way, when I heard they were sending someone to abduct you before Dante's men got to you. In my hurry to convince my boss by volunteering my services, I collected only the bare bone details of the ongoing game. As far as I know, Dante either wanted you killed or taken. Since I knew where you were and had excellent alternate plans, and the fact that my boss' wife owed me a favor, I got to save your ass. Satisfied now?"

There was a short silence as Svenni digested the information.

"You could have told me this yesterday," he finally said.

"Agreed. But try to see it from my point of view. I've looked forward to having you for three years and I was this close to getting my vacation dreams fulfilled. Then this comes up. So I stepped into the bar. See you there waiting for a quick fuck and not with me. I lost my head a bit." Martin recalled his quick anger. "You know what happened after that. We got distracted."

"Yeah, by sex and bullets."

"Is it all sex to you, then?" Martin had braced himself for rejection but somehow, the idea of Svenni not seeing him as more than casual sex made him feel...hurt. But what had he expected? "Nothing more?"

Svenni gave him a quick glance, his blue eyes filled with mockery. "Well, I thought at the time it was. Then you told me your dick came with an island vacation. I don't know. Does that sound casual to you?"

Relief expanded in Martin's chest. He hadn't realized how important this had become for him till now. "I usually don't plan for three-year casual," he noted, his voice low.

"Yeah, I don't think I can wait another three years for whatever you have in mind," Svenni said, wryly. "This game stuff. I'm somehow tangled in it and I'm glad you saved me from Dante, but it isn't over yet. I'm sure he's still after me."

"Which makes sense why you can't go back to your old life as yet. You must go into hiding anyway. It's a good time for a vacation, right?"

Svenni rewarded him with one of his mischievous crooked smiles that always made his gut tighten. "The Knight and his Pawn. That sounds like a totally kinky romance novel."

Martin laughed. It was so like Svenni to make fun of everything. It was going to be a fun time getting to know each other. If they made it to the island alive. A sobering thought. "Jaan didn't say much. He wanted me to know Dante hurt you all those years ago before you escaped."

He was very careful with his choice of words. The words Jaan used were 'tortured' and 'played with.' He looked on silently, noting the other man's rigid shoulders and grim expression. A quick calculation had told him Svenni must have been only eighteen or nineteen at that time; one carried one's memories larger than life from that time, especially the bad ones.

"Did Jaan tell—"

"No, he didn't reveal anything, so don't get pissed off at him. He wanted me to know how much you hated Dante. It's his way of telling me to keep you safe."

"Fucking hell. I'm not helpless. I've been keeping me safe since I was a kid," Svenni grated out. His hands slammed the steering wheel. "I wish Jaan had kept his trap shut."

"You asked me what he told me. Fucking stop losing your temper at everyone, will you? You're so goddamn prickly all the time. Forget pawn. More like 'The Knight and the Hedgehog'."

His attempt to lighten the mood worked. Svenni looked startled for a second, then burst out in laughter. That infectious sound had always attracted him. It was sweet and a complete contrast to the gutter mouth that came with the quick temper. It was like a promise—wild, passionate, rough sex and sweet surrender afterwards.

A minute later, Svenni turned off the highway and drove to a stop at a rest area. He turned off the engine. Took a deep breath. A bitter tweak lifted the corners of his sensuous mouth.

His voice was flat, emotionless. "The beating wasn't great but I took it. Part of the price of getting caught. I was even prepared about getting killed if I didn't think of something soon. It's all a jumble of memories now—the pain, the panic, mixed with ten kinds of fear. Being that young was like being a little crazy. Dante had his map back but he wanted to make sure I hadn't studied or remembered anything. I'd played the dumb young thief pretty well, I thought, but he was fucking suspicious and wanted to test me. His starving me didn't get me to admit to remembering anything. His beatings just made me weak. Sure, like I said, I was fucking crazy too. I mocked him. I told him I would admit to fucking anything if he kept torturing me, so what was the point? Just kill me already, right? I thought I was going to die when he gagged me and took out a knife. I remember I was even mentally saying some kind of prayer." Svenni rubbed his face wearily with one hand. "That was when he brought in the girl. She was just a kid."

Martin put a gentle hand on Svenni's shoulder. "You don't have to tell me anything else," he said, trying to keep his anger from showing. He'd been in several rescue missions in which he'd seen the results of torture. Christ, but he hadn't been eighteen or nineteen, though. "Sooner or later, someone will finish off the sick bastard."

"Right. It's only been a fucking decade. How many do you think he's tortured all these years?" Svenni's voice was suddenly fierce, his blue eyes bright with emotion. "Do you know why he gagged me? Because he knew I was going to scream out everything I knew while he was...slicing that...poor kid. The gag was his punishment. I couldn't save her because he couldn't hear anything I confessed. At that point, it was too late, you see. He made me responsible for her death. And I hate myself—"

Martin grabbed Svenni under the chin. "You are not responsible," he thundered. "Christ, how can you blame yourself for—"

"Her blood is on my hands!"

"You were bound and gagged! You think he hadn't done that before, that he wouldn't have killed other children?"

"If I had told him what I've seen of that damn map, I might be dead, but she could have lived!"

"For how much longer? How do you know whether her fate wouldn't have been the same? Except you would be dead, along with her. You were scarcely a kid yourself, remember? Nineteen isn't twenty-nine. That bastard's kink is destroying children and childhood. You're a victim, Svenni." Martin gave the mutinous mouth a hard kiss. "Mourn, yes. Be angry, yes. But I'm not going to let you blame yourself again."

"Who the fuck do you think you are?" Svenni slapped his hands hard against Martin's chest. "I only confided in you because...damn it, I can't believe I confided in you."

Ignoring the pain radiating from his chest from the unexpected push, Martin noted Svenni hadn't knocked away the hand under his chin. He leaned closer. "I'm glad you did, hedgehog."

He locked his mouth firmly on Svenni's. He'd wanted to be gentle because this moment was meant to be something special, a sharing of confidences and a bonding of their relationship, but he also recognized his new lover's defense mechanism. Svenni had reacted to this past trauma by denying himself, by not letting himself see anything meaningful in his life. Dangerous situations only made him more foolhardy.

So Martin offered what was needed—someone who would let Svenni surrender without feeling guilty. He didn't mind that at all. He'd always felt strangely protective of him and was touched and humbled at the new trust given to him.

Svenni was responding fiercely, tongue and teeth devouring his mouth, his hands moving up over his pecs to squeeze his shoulders, and then upwards through his hair. If there wasn't a plastic console between them, Martin would've been all over him in a second, small space be damned.

When the kiss ended, they were both breathing hard. Martin's cock strained against his pants. Their foreheads rested against each other's.

"We can't seem to stop being hot and heavy about each other long enough to have a decent argument," Svenni panted, his hand deliberately reaching lower for a teasing caress.

"A predicament," Martin agreed. "We must really get serious about fighting. I'll arrange for wrestling mats for our vacation house."

Svenni's body shook with mirth and Martin was glad he was helping him to forget his sorrow. He ran his fingers through the wild blond mane, unruly and beautiful, just like its owner.

"I'm okay now. We can get back on the road," Svenni said, straightening up. He gathered his hair back with a tie. "Hey, thanks. Sorry for hitting your wound. I forgot."

"Not a problem." Martin reluctantly returned to a more comfortable position. "Just don't beat yourself up again. You do that, I might have to make hot and heavy our frequent agenda."

Svenni's lips curled at the promise as he turned the car on. "You know what? I'm thinking these last wild and crazy forty-eight hours *is* the vacation. Kinky sex. Fighting off bad guys. A six foot five handsome bastard with a big dick at my beck and call. It *has* been kind of fun."

Branson laughed. Only his reckless Scandinavian hedgehog would think being shot at as a fun holiday. Wild and crazy indeed. And so hotly sweet in bed. Except for the flying bullets part, he looked forward to many more of the same ahead.

* * *

Svenni had to admit, life was more interesting with Martin Branson around. More colorful. Less lonely. The man was an intriguing mix of guard dog, hot pillaging Viking pirate and Chinese ivory puzzle ball. He grinned at the analogy.

Yeah, he was all protective and demanding on the outside, but like the beautiful and mysterious Chinese puzzle ball, he had delicate layers underneath, all cleverly hidden away and difficult to solve. It'd take time to explore each layer....

He took the last turn directed by the GPS and saw the private airstrip ahead. They'd arrived.

Branson sat up, scanning the surroundings. He pulled out his cell phone.

"Plane ID, please," he said. "Password, please. Everything on schedule."

"So strange. Isn't it supposed to be the other way round, you giving the password?" Svenni asked when Branson finished the call.

Branson grinned. "It's like a reversed knock-knock joke."

"What's that?"

"Say 'knock, knock.'"

"Knock, knock," Svenni said.

"Who's there?"

Uh? Svenni was stuck for a quick answer. Oh. He gave Branson another sideways glance. "That's so lame."

"Got you, didn't it? Turn to the right there. We can park in that hangar."

Svenni pulled into the hangar. It was large and very well-lit. He took note of the surroundings—three men carrying stuff on the ramp above, three talking nearby, one of whom gave their arrival an acknowledging wave. "I've never been on a private jet before. Do you fly?"

"I have a license but this isn't my jet. Or my property."

Svenni sighed as they got out of the car. "Damn. Here I thought I scored a big, rich boyfriend." At the sound of a squealing tire wheels, he looked behind them. Outside, a Jeep screamed into view, picking up speed as it approached. "Umm, Martin? Men with guns."

"Get down!" A voice from above yelled.

A body fell from the ramp above, landing near them in a thud. Svenni felt Branson's hand on his shoulder, pushing him down on the ground. Someone activated the hangar entrance and it began sliding down. Gunfire echoed in the huge space. Running feet and shouts. A bullet hit another vehicle beside him.

Svenni rolled under the car. Where the hell did Branson go?

He peered out from where he was. Everyone was scrambling. The hangar door appeared to be stuck because it wasn't descending any more. The jeep was charging at them at full speed now. From nowhere, another vehicle came like a bullet train from the side and rammed right near the back wheel. Brakes squealed as the driver of the hit vehicle tried to stay upright. A few of the passengers had been thrown off. Screams of pain added to the cacophony of vehicles hitting metal supports.

He needed to get to his gun in his car. Crawling out, he managed to get the door open before another bullet shattered the window. He ducked inside, punching at the middle console container to get it to open, cursing when his fist hit a stray piece of glass.

He pulled out his weapon and darted a quick look through the back windshield. Bah. Too much stuff in the way. Couldn't see a damn thing. He got out of his crouched position in the car and using the door as a shield, looked towards the area where the two vehicles had come to a stop.

From the corner of his eye, Svenni caught two men in hand-to-hand combat. One of them was Branson, his tall and imposing figure delivering a blow which the other blocked. The other fighter's back looked familiar and Svenni winced as he elbowed Branson in the midriff. They were moving too much for him for a shot. Svenni surveyed the rest of the scene.

There were men on top of each other, pounding away. A few sprawled unmoving on the ground. There were the two vehicles piled together like scrapped metal, with men fighting there too. Svenni couldn't figure out who was on which side. It looked as if they were all trying to kill each other.

Movement to his left. He caught sight of a man aiming his weapon at Branson and his opponent. It didn't look as if he was waiting for a winner of that fight. Svenni took aim and pulled the trigger. The man toppled over.

A deep-throated war cry sounded. He turned to his right. A huge thug was charging towards him from a few feet away. With a machete.

"Oh shit!" Svenni ducked behind the car door.

He heard a loud clang and the door shook from the blow. The plastic arm rest hit his head several times. The force of the blow pushed hard against the door, forcing him to jump out of its way or have part of his body crushed. Half lying down, he looked up. His assailant was pulling at his weapon, readying for another blow.

Oh shit. His gun lay a few feet away. He lunged for it. The machete landed right where his body had been, taking out small chunks of concrete.

He fired his gun. The thug kept coming, body bent forward, menacingly swinging the blade.

He fired again. Nothing. Out of ammo.

In desperation, Svenni kicked at the car door which was still slightly ajar. It swung open wide, the top of the window smacking the throat area of his enemy. The other man grunted and took a few steps back, one hand holding his injured windpipe.

Svenni got up and slid across the boot of his car to the other side. The attacker gave chase.

Why, why, why did everyone get a bad guy with a gun and he got one with a fucking machete? The ridiculous question zipped through his mind as he ran further back into the hangar. Weapon. He needed a weapon. He pushed one of those tool carts on wheels around and charged straight at machete guy.

Wham! Body, cart, machete came together, tools spilling left and right, and Svenni felt the smash-up from his arms to his upper back. His teeth clattered from the jarring force. The other man's big body spilled over the top side of the cart, his weapon pointing dangerously close to Svenni's crotch.

Svenni skipped out of the way. Then kicked at the hand holding the machete.

"Let go already, will ya?" he yelled, then kicked the goon's head for good measure.

He turned. And his forehead came up against cold steel. Fuck. This time it *was* a gun.

"No!" Svenni heard Branson's voice boomed from behind his new assailant.

"Relax, old son. I don't mean to kill your lover boy here. That's why he was assigned to non-bullet status."

"Dimitri?" Svenni asked, astonished. Last person he'd expected. Non-bullet status? Oh, that accounted for the machete.

"Let him go, D."

Dimitri shook his head. Still pointing his gun at his target, he walked forward and positioned himself to face both Svenni and Branson. "Sorry, Brando. He's coming with me. I learned there's a huge price on his head from your attackers this morning. Something to do with a treasure. That sounds intriguing."

"Like running the streets of Tallinn isn't enough any more?" Branson asked. His gaze was steady. "You okay, Svenni? Did the machete get you?"

"Tsk. So much concern. I'm jealous."

Svenni frowned. Was Dimitri an ex-lover of Branson? "I'm okay. Flesh wound," he said aloud.

"What exactly do you want, D?"

"I went through a lot of trouble for you. Damages at my bar. Then smashed a whole brand new SUV to get those guys coming at you in their Jeep. The person wants Jorgensen here so badly, he's sending teams after the two of you. I thought I needed my damages paid. Either Jorgensen's head or treasure ought to do it, right? From my interrogation, it looks like the treasure isn't quite found yet, so hey, I'll settle for the money on Jorgensen's head then." He turned to look at Svenni. "Not literally, mind you. I told my man your head must stay attached."

"Glad to know," Svenni said, dryly.

"I'll pay for the damages," Branson offered. "Just let him go."

"You see, you're too damn interested in him. You're forgetting our spec. ops. lessons, Brando, son. Never show the other party your weakness. Blond boy here is a weakness, dude."

Svenni noted how Dimitri's usual accent had seamlessly slipped into American. He'd known Dimitri long enough to have a vague idea about the man's background. He and Branson were roughly the same age, early to mid-thirties. Could it be Dimitri served with Branson in some kind of military outfit before?

"So our history doesn't mean a thing any more?" Branson asked, taking a step closer.

"Uh-uh. Stay where you are. I'll shoot your sweetheart here if I have to. Look, we were good friends, so you can offer me a deal. What do you have to persuade me to let him back into your arms? Cash is nice but the other side's got plenty of cash too."

Dimitri's tone was mocking, meant to egg Branson into doing something foolish. Svenni looked at Branson, standing so still. He wasn't afraid of Dimitri; the man had as much said he didn't want to kill him. But the longer the standstill, the more dangerous the situation would become.

* * *

H-A-X, Hostage/Arms Exchange, was familiar territory for Martin. He'd been sent by Knights, Inc., to negotiate deals between enemies before, playing middleman to arms, humans, or any contractual obligations between the two parties. Sometimes it involved governments, sometimes, parents and kidnap victims, sometimes, two warring tribal lords.

An H-A-X had basic ingredients. Emotional value. Bargaining power. A cunning eye for negotiation through dangerous waters.

He emptied his mind of all the basic emotions he'd seen on the sides of the ones losing most in this kind of situation—fear, panic, hope, eagerness. Fear and panic gave power to the other side. Hope destroyed the ability to see what the other side was doing. And eagerness to hurry the deal created unfair advantages.

He was in a position of weakness. But he'd been here before. Position of weakness could be forged into one of advantage. He just had to be careful he didn't sacrifice too much.

His emotional value was Dimitri's and his past friendship. His bargaining chip was his knowledge of how D.'s mind worked. And yeah, D was a dangerous man, but not as cunning as he thought.

"I thought that was why you retired, D," Martin said. "Remember your complaints? Action that brings in cash, you don't want the glory, you said, you want the money? From what I've seen, you have plenty, so you're lying here. Your status on the streets of Tallinn brings you all the cash you'll ever need."

Dimitri shrugged. "Ya got me. I'm getting bored. All the money, some action, but no real action, buddy. None like the kind you and I saw way back when. And I can't just rejoin now. Fucking way too old and I'm neck deep in my shit." He shrugged again. "What's an old soldier like me to do, eh? Your little adventure at my place brought back some good memories, Brando baby. You and me and our men, right?"

"Since when have we ever lived in the past?" Martin scoffed. "We make our lives, remember? You got what you wanted and now you want more, is that it?"

"I want what you got, Bran."

Martin made sure he made eye contact with Dimitri. Had to keep him focus on their friendship. "You sure about that?" he drawled. "There's not that much cash and it's mostly all about running covert teams. You were tired of that shit before you took off. Besides, you're kind of dependent on your hired hands now. My work is mostly done alone."

Dimitri spat on the ground. "Are you challenging me, asshole? We fought just now. Tell me I've lost a step."

Martin smiled. "One. Okay, maybe half. You need training again, that's all." He thumbed behind him. "You want in on the game, you take your thugs off my guys. You secure the ones in the Jeep. Then we talk. What do you say?" When Dimitri's eyes narrowed, he added softly, "You can keep that weapon pointed at my weakness, if you're nervous about me trying anything."

Dimitri laughed then snapped out in Estonian. Martin could hear the people behind him following his orders. Good. Step One accomplished. He dared to look at Svenni then. His "weakness" winked at him.

Martin kept his poker face on, but inside, he started to worry. Svenni was the unpredictable ingredient here. He had no doubt, right now, the man was thinking of some risky ideas. He could only hope he could get the negotiations all worked out before things started happening.

"My men are taking care of your enemies. That's my first favor. Your turn," Dimitri said, his weapon still loosely pointing near the back of Svenni's head.

Martin showed his hands, then very slowly took a step forward. "Treasure hunts. They call it The Game. There are people—groups—around the world in The Game. If you want in, you'll have to put aside time, money and curb your usual impatience."

Dimitri cocked his head. "Bored rich people chasing treasures. Really, Martin."

Martin shrugged. "Rich people need some excitement too. My outfit gets hired out for parts of their so-called quests." He nodded at Svenni. "I'm to deliver him to my boss. You give him to me, I'll give you the first clue that would put you ahead of most of the others. That's my favor. Your turn."

"How would I know what you're telling is the truth? And why the fuck would I want to go treasure hunting?"

"You don't. But that's your risk. You're bored, you said. And you've got money. Maybe you're like those rich folks, needing some excitement." Martin took another step forward. "I have the clue in my pocket. You can have it, D. Think of all the options you have. You can sell it to the highest bidder. Get hired like me to go chasing after other clues. Form your own group and go all Indiana Jones, if you feel like leaving Tallinn for a while. Almost like old times, right?"

"Yeah, but you won't be with me. Come with me. We can drop this fuck boy off anywhere you want."

"Hey!" Svenni interrupted. "He's mine, asshole."

It was difficult, but Martin stopped the smile forming on his lips. Dimitri was liable to make life difficult if he decided it'd slow Martin down. Much as he loved Svenni's possessive declaration, he chose to ignore him for now.

"Come on, D, think about it. We'll kill each other after a few days. I'd be insisting on running the team my way and you won't take orders. Better you go on your own and try to get to the goods before I do."

"True. And I'm a better hunter than you. You recall how I always find all the landmines?"

Martin nodded. Dimitri had an uncanny instinct when it came to hidden stuff. He thrived on challenges. "Yeah. But you're out of practice and I have more experience now."

"Yeah?"

"Yeah."

"You're on. Give me the damn clue."

Showing his empty hand, he reached in his shirt pocket and pulled out the small artifact he'd earlier shown Svenni. It was an antique so Dimitri would be fooled into thinking he had the real thing, but it was a copy of the really ancient genuine article. The Temple was probably not going to be happy about this but he would do anything to get Svenni out of harm's way.

"That's it? What the hell is that? I thought it'd be a treasure map."

"A clue. Maybe to the map. Maybe to the treasure. I haven't figured it out yet. Nor has those fuckers after Jorgensen and my asses. Do you want it? Fair exchange—your prisoner for this clue."

There were a few seconds of silence as Dimitri thought about it. Then he nodded. He nudged Svenni with his gun and they moved the few steps forward. His free hand reached out and grabbed the artifact. At the same time, he pointed his weapon at Martin.

Martin had expected the unexpected, especially from his favorite risk taker. He'd also expected D to play dirty. He dove sideways. At the same time, he caught sight of Svenni pushing Dimitri's hand out of the way as the gun fired. His heart leapt into his throat as he watched them struggle. Dimitri's fist glanced at Svenni's jaw. Svenni headbutted Dimitri. The weapon went off again.

Martin jumped to his feet just as Svenni dealt a vicious swipe at his opponent, his blond hair swinging loose from its tie. He wasn't sure what happened but the result was immediate. Dimitri crumpled to the ground.

There was a huge commotion as Dimitri's men realize what had just happened. A quick lookaround told Martin his guards at the hangar had it under control this time, or mostly in control. There were more of them than he'd counted at their arrival, which was good news, because they were going to have their hands full sorting out which of their prisoners belong to whom. They would be waiting for further instructions on how to handle them, so Dimitri and his men would be delayed until his say so. He gave a nod to the pilot who then started to run toward the plane, followed by two others.

Martin ran toward Svenni, who was dusting off his hands, a big triumphant smile on his lips. "Fucker," he was saying. "I'll show you what this fuck boy is capable of."

"What the hell did you do?" Martin demanded. *There was blood on his lips and his hand was bleeding.* "Are you all right?"

Not waiting for an answer and with no time for explanations, he scooped the other man up over one shoulder—not unlike the first time at the bar—and made a run toward the plane.

"Hey!" Svenni yelled.

Martin ignored everything but getting on the plane. There were just too many bad guys around and the sooner they were in the air—and alone—the better. The plane was ready by the time he reached the steps.

"Go, go, go!"

He ran up and deposited his man inside, out of the way of stray bullets and...a fist met the side of his chin. He stared at Svenni, who was shaking his injured hand.

"What the hell!" Martin rubbed his bruised jaw. "What's that for?"

"You can't just keep carrying me off! I have legs."

"You're bleeding!"

"That's from my hand. I cut myself on glass!"

"How was I to know? I just see blood all over you. There wasn't time. We needed to go!" Martin yelled back.

"Seat belts, gentleman," a voice said over the intercom. "This is going to be rough if they give chase."

"They won't unless Dimitri gives the order and he's...how did you knock him out?" Martin asked. "You're still bleeding. Let me look at your hand."

"Will you stop?" Svenni walked over to a seat. "All my stuff is in my car, dammit...man, this plane is nice. Check out the space! I guess I'd better try to stop bleeding all over the carpet."

Martin pulled out a hanky. "Here. I'll go look for a kit up front." He looked up as a man appeared holding an emergency kit and a wash cloth "Thanks."

"Sir, headquarters wants you to contact them as soon as we leave the ground."

"Got it. Can you close the compartment for privacy after takeoff, please?"

"Yes, sir."

Sitting down in front of Svenni, he took the latter's hand in his to examine the cut. Svenni wasn't even paying him any attention, turning his head left and right as he checked the luxury cabin out, his mouth hanging open. He understood the feeling. For a first timer, private jet travel was something to behold. There weren't any narrow seats or people crammed together like sardines. This particular jet was tastefully furnished, with a huge table at the back end for conferencing and a large screen TV. There was a sofa and even a kitchen for a chef to cook a personalized meal.

"How did you cut yourself on glass?" Martin asked as he cleansed the wound with iodine.

"That reminds me. You owe me a fucking car too," Svenni told him.

Martin shook his head. "That mouth of yours," he murmured. "We'll get your things sent, all right? No big deal. There, all cleaned up. What color band-aid do you want? There's one striped purple and yellow, there's rainbow, and oh look, one with cute bows printed on it."

Svenni sighed. "You're teasing me again."

"Nope. I think the owner of this jet just has a sense of humor. Or maybe they bought these for their kids. Which do you want? I kind of like the one with bows." He grinned again at Svenni's hard stare. "No? You want the striped one? What's your decision?"

"I'm trying to decide whether to hit you again or kiss you."

Ah, the adrenaline was doing its job, giving them both a hard-on. Martin felt his smile grow wider. "Tell you what. While you decide, let me make that call to the boss. After that, I'm all yours to beat up on. Here's a towel for the cracked lip. I'd rather not taste blood if you decide on kissing instead."

* * *

Svenni looked out the cabin window. He could get used to this. Idly, he played with the idea of stealing a jet like this one and hiding it. But then he'd need to learn how to fly one. Or, he glanced at the man in front of him, find someone who could.

He'd thought he knew Martin Branson. He'd sought—used up his own savings—to buy information about him. Yet, two days with this man and he'd come to the realization there was so much more than the details in a file. His lover was an intense man with a lot of experience. He already knew Branson was a military type, probably great on the battlefield, but from watching him handle Dimitri, he'd shown an ability to think on his feet in the middle of danger. A tough and yet, seductive, leader. A man who knew what he wanted and went after it.

So damn sexy.

Svenni had an idea of how it would be like in a relationship with such a man. He'd always had a weakness for someone to take charge sexually. It was a fantasy because being a bigger man, he had to pretend a lot in bed.

He studied Tall, Dark and Sexy sitting across from him, fiddling with his phone. *No need to pretend with him,* his voice whispered in his mind. And he shivered with anticipation inside.

"Who are you calling now?" Svenni asked.

"John and Kel. They've probably been updated about our...little adventure and will need a quick debriefing on my status." He winked at Svenni. "It's a long ride to the next stop."

Svenni gave him a light kick. "You know what? I'm probably going to nap all the way there."

"We can convert this into a bed, you know. I can show you...umm...yes, it's me, Kel, and I'm A-OK. A small distraction. We're going to need some clean up back there and some compensation for some...ah...damages." Branson leaned back in his seat. "I'll update you on Dimitri. He isn't really a hostile...yet. I used to know him well. I had to do a H-A-X and give him the artifact in exchange for Svenni Jorgensen. He'll be contacting people soon, I'd imagine, to find out more about The Game. I know how his mind works. He wants to find the treasure before me because that's how competitive he was when we battled together. But can you get the orders out to hang on to him and his men for a day or so?"

Svenni kept quiet, listening to Branson's deep voice as the latter gave a rundown on the whole situation. As suspected, Dimitri and he had history together, but how much? Dimitri didn't appear to have hard feelings. In fact, at the bar, if he recalled correctly, he'd just laughed when Branson had carried him off.

"Yes, you really have to take care of whoever is leaking info at your end, Kel. Let John handle it. I mean, he isn't too busy honeymooning, right?" Branson grinned at whatever was said on the other end. "Right. Of course. Can you send more security for our arrival? I just don't feel like another run-in with Dante's thugs after a long plane ride....what? Hmm. Well, ye...ah."

The long drawl caught Svenni's attention. Branson winked at him.

"I don't know. Do I have to play bodyguard? It's supposed to be my vacation, you know. I need pay if work is involved." Branson continued. "How long? All right. I'll do it as long as you stop thinking of using him as a pawn." He laughed. "I'm not telling you my next move, my Queen-to-be. I'm not that stupid. But I *could* do a H-A-X with you—him for what he told me about the cuneiform markings. Ha, knew you'd be interested. I'll update my status soon."

Svenni looked back at Branson when he rang off. There was that hungry gleam again, the look that seemed to be able to look deep inside him and see what he wanted. The shiver of anticipation jolted in his gut again.

"Looks like there's a change of plans," Branson said. "They need to find the leak first. If we show up, we're liable to get more attacks because for some reason, you're important."

"So what's next?"

"I've been ordered to go on my vacation." Branson laughed. "So, we're taking off to that island once we arrive at our layover. I'll fly us there and no one without top clearance will know. You, me, sun, fun."

Svenni frowned. "You mentioned being a bodyguard."

"Well, that's what they want me to do, be your bodyguard." Branson lazily propped his legs next to Svenni. "I'll guard your body like it's a treasure."

Svenni put his hand on Branson's knee. "What about that treasure hunt? The one you tempted Dimitri with? Don't you want to be in the chase so you can beat him?"

Branson watched the progress of his hand with interest. "I have time. I need time to rest up after my own long game. If you're interested," his voice lowered as Svenni deliberately moved his hand higher, "and if you aren't too occupied, we can do some of the prep work while...sunning."

"What prep work?" Svenni asked.

"Not as fun as what you're currently prepping," Branson said, his voice getting huskier. "But I'd like to get a look at that online game your data-miner is playing, maybe start a character in it. We could also do some...research...on the cuneiform figures you memorized from the treasure map."

"Research. Prep work. Sounds exciting," Svenni agreed. "We can even wrestle in between all the sunning and funning and prepping."

"What exactly did you do to Dimitri, anyway? One moment he and you were fighting and the next, he was out like a light. I know he's a better fighter than that."

"Oh, it was nothing. See this?"

Branson frowned at the bracelet Svenni was wearing. "Yeah."

"That's the present from Jaan. Check this out." Svenni flicked his wrist in a certain motion. A vicious-looking needle popped out. "It has a sleeping agent at the tip. Jaan gave it to me in case Dante caught me again. It can only be used once, unfortunately." He met Branson's wide eyes and added, "Served the fucker right, insulting me and trying to shoot you."

"You...gave up your possible means of escape for me?" He asked quietly.

Svenni nodded. Before he could say another word, he was hauled off his seat onto Branson's warm chest.

There was a long silence. When Branson was through with him, Svenni said breathlessly, "Let's convert that bed and do some prep work."

THE END

Dear Reader,

Thank you for buying my books. I'm starting this series of individual short stories/episodes so I can add different accounts of spy adventures, including vignettes of the earlier life of the popular Jed McNeil's (Number Nine from the Commando series) and hero of Virtually His and Virtually Hers.

Excerpt from **TEMPTING TROUBLE**

Grace moaned. Something was doing horribly erotic things to her ear, darting in and out, exploring, swirling, seducing. She tried to twist away from its sexual probing, but found she couldn't move. Hands moved over her body, lips seared her skin. He was good, she thought, fighting off sleep, so clever with that tongue, so strong and tender and—she let out a scream—horribly wet. Cold water dripped down her back and legs. She forced her eyes open, still half asleep, expecting to confront some nightmarish creature frothing at the mouth, dripping all over her.

She was close. It was Lance Mercy in her bed, on her, holding her down. And he was wet from head to toe. His eyes were blazing like those of a wild beast on the attack.

Grace closed her eyes and opened them again, willing her nightmare to go away. It wasn't one. He was still there in person. She shrieked again, trying to sit up. "How did you get in here?" Her panicked voice was hushed, husky from alcohol and sleep.

Lance sat astride her, studying her wakening horror with renewed amusement. He did like getting back at her for making him feel jealous. "Some doors can't be dead-bolted, sweetheart," he drawled.

She frowned, then remembered her sliding door. She called him an extremely unflattering name.

"Tsk, tsk, such language from that pretty mouth," he chided.

"You're wet!" She squirmed. "Get off, you...oaf!"

"I'm sorry. Here, let me get out of these wet clothes."

Grace's eyes widened, as she slowly comprehended his meaning. Her mouth tasted like cotton as she watched him pull his wet shirt off and toss it carelessly over his shoulder. His chest muscles were taut, revealing his mood, the movement of his bare arms tense and deliberate. She started to tremble when his hands reached for the buttons of his pants. She tried to speak but her tongue seemed to have disappeared, her eyes wildly following his hands. Finally, she just shook her head at him.

But Lance wasn't in the mood. "You got wet from my clothes, sweetheart. Let me help you take them off." He held on to the front of her maroon outfit and with one savage tug, tore it down almost to her waist.

Grace came alive, rearing up and catching him by surprise, pushing him off. Rolling off the bed, she scrambled out of the room, almost killing herself with only one high heel on. He hopped off and followed closely.

"Don't think you're going to come in here and find me soft and pliant after the way you acted out there!" Grace fumed, hobbling backwards from him.

"You didn't expect me to be in the best of moods after the act you pulled at the function, did you?" He stalked her as she used the sofa as a buffer between them. "Did you?"

"Did I do anything you told me not to?" she challenged.

"Yes!" he hissed, walking around the sofa. She half-ran, half-stumbled to the nearby chaise lounge. "I told you not to interfere."

"You told me to stay out of the way," she corrected, "which I did. I kept my bloody word, so stop glaring at me! What, do you have any complaints? Didn't you accomplish your mission?"

Using one arm, Lance vaulted over the sofa. Grace hastily retreated away from the chaise, trying to think of a way to calm a savage beast. Half-naked, his hair darkened by the rain, eyes blazing, he didn't look anything like the suave deputy advisor to the Council of Asian Trade. Her heart thumped against her throat at the dangerous look in his eyes.

"You're right, I did accomplish my mission," he informed her, his eyes level, "and now I've come to accomplish my other one."

She swallowed. "What's that?" She stared at him as he kept advancing.

"I told you we would celebrate tonight." He indicated the empty bottle on the coffee table. "Seems like you started without me."

Grace's back bumped into the sliding door that led to the balcony. "I wanted to be alone," she told him, still defiant.

"And I told you I would be back later." He was close enough to grab her. "Did you have any doubts I would?"

"Yes! I don't want you here!" She turned, slid open the glass door, and ran out into the rain.

She was dead meat. Lance followed her, cornering her against the banister. Rain half-blinded her as he twined his fingers in her wet hair, pulling her face up to meet his.

"You have a hearing problem, love. I also told you," he said over the drumming of the rain around them, "that game time is over, Grace. I meant it."

****

About the Author

Gennita Low writes sexy military and techno spy-fi romance. She also co-owns a roof construction business and knows 600 ways to kill with roofing tools as well as yell at her workers in five languages. A three-time Golden Heart finalist, her first book, Into Danger, about a SEAL out-of-water, won the Romantic Times Reviewers Choice Award for Best Romantic Intrigue. Besides her love for SEALs, she works with an Airborne Ranger who taught her all about mental toughness and physical endurance. Gennita lives in Florida with her mutant poms and one chubby squirrel.

You can email Gennita at Jenn@Gennita-Low.com. To learn more about Gennita, visit:
www.Gennita-Low.com,
www.rooferauthor.blogspot.com   and
www.facebook.com/gennita

www.ingramcontent.com/pod-product-compliance
Lightning Source LLC
Chambersburg PA
CBHW030613130626
46552CB00002B/543